# Dancing In The Dust

# **<u>Chapter One</u>**

The hard baked dirt cracks ever so slightly beneath the soles of my feet as I shift the bike's weight to set it on its stand. It's been a hot summer. I loosen my goggles, slide them over my brow and pull down my snood, wiping the dust absentmindedly, simultaneously. An unconscious practice now. Forget to regularly wipe the dust and before you know it the layers are cracking on your cheeks as it combines with your sweat, stiffening into a mask that will tear every hair out of your skin as you try to remove it. Once you've experienced that a few times, wiping the dust becomes as automatic as breathing.

I can't explain the dust. The other horrors, seeming plagues and oddities, I can almost or mostly explain to myself. But the dust? Is it connected to the plague? It crept in during that first month, first a fine layer, lightly coating every surface, almost sticky, like wet sand but finer. It was hard to escape and the layers grew thicker as the populace thinned. Is it just a random side effect of this disease that swallowed most of the life on our once abundant planet, or a natural consequence of the calamitous changes among which we now live?

I haven't figured it out yet.

Give me a break, my resources on that front are pretty limited. Mostly relying on old fashioned powers of deduction and what education I gleaned up to age sixteen. The books in the house I would have to flee have been pretty valuable in keeping me alive, but were hardly for the scientific minded. More useful for learning 101 ways to kill, eat and utilise a badger. Shame we don't see many of those anymore.

The sunlight seems like it should pierce my eyes, facing west as I am near the setting of the day. It bothers me much less these days. In the same way that I rarely find the need to light my way at night anymore. My eyes adjust so well now. Oddities...curiosities. Fun to collect in this dusty dystopia.

I slow my breath and close my eyes, listening for the sounds of the gang I've been tracking these past three days. I've deliberately stopped and set my bike a few miles back from them. I can see from their tracks left in the dust, the way the wind has only slightly blurred the edges, that they passed through here less than fifteen minutes ago. No one is driving faster than fifteen miles an hour on these roads, unless they're lucky enough, or ingenious enough, to have a bike like mine that can easily weave through obstacles. I estimate them to be around four miles away. Sound travels far in this desolate landscape and my ears can pick up the slightest susurration after so many years of silent solitude. At least, that's my best explanation for being able to hear a lizard drink at a river a mile away. Hearing these uncouth fools setting up their camp is a doddle.

Ok, that might be a touch of hyperbole. But I did once track a deer nearly half a mile away by the sound of it lapping at a pond and shifting its weight.

I could have taken them the first night, catching up was never the issue. It's always prudent though, to take time to observe numbers, habits, discipline, leadership structure, that sort of thing. You don't see much originality in how these gangs operate. While there seemed to be no rhyme or reason to how the plague claimed its victims, there was a clear rationale for surviving the massacres that followed. The strong survived. The weak perished, or were enslaved - If they were pretty enough, or young enough. No one is all that pretty anymore. Not too many bright sparks remaining either, at least as I've observed it. Humanity will continue to wither without my assistance. These days though, there is precious little to entertain me, and I enjoy tearing violent men down to size.

*

I set down my rucksack. Time to tool up. I pull out my gloves, elbow and knee pads, and boot mods. I admire each item as I reveal them. A lot of time went into these pieces. The aforementioned deer ultimately served me well.

I hadn't intended on killing it initially. There were plenty of other food sources remaining, even with the near extinction of warm blooded creatures, and this was the first deer I'd seen in nearly eight years. I wondered as I crept closer why the deer had yet to startle and flee. I'd snapped the odd branch and dislodged a stone or two in my haste to set eyes on the creature. Through small gaps in the foliage set a few meters back from the edge of the pond I could see the deer's haunches. Still no sign of movement, though I still heard it lapping away. Could it be that this animal had never encountered predatory life? Precious little remains after all that could threaten it.

Standing to my full height, unimpressive as it is, (at least compared to the large men I encounter in my hunts) I took in the creature, this miraculous, living, warm blooded mammal. I allowed my eyes to take in its greyish brown coat, roam over the sunlight dappling its flanks and shoulders, dust coating the dull hooves and antlers. I sighed and stood still, allowing the wonder of the moment to envelope me. A joyous wonder is such a rarity in our new world. A predictable horror is far more common.

A dull, dark blob caught my attention, marring the smooth perfection. I narrowed my gaze and looked more closely at its rear left hoof. Dried blood, mixed with the ever present dust. I moved slowly, smoothly, around the rear of the deer, to better see the wound. I could see now the listless way its head hung, the bones protruding from its chest and shoulders. The muscle wastage. I flanked the deer and stopped in my tracks. Fucking rattlesnakes! Judging by the torn flesh and number of bite marks, this deer either disturbed several snakes or really, really pissed one off. The concentration of bites suggested one, furious, danger noodle.

The deer turned its head to look at me over its shoulder, eyes dull, that beautiful deep brown appearing filmed over. A few flies crawled over its muzzle and eyes, and more clustered thickly around the wound site. Even if he knew that I might have posed a danger, the poor beast was far beyond caring. He turned back to the water, lapping with what little energy he had. Snake bite thirst is a serious business. The wounds looked massively infected. The smell alone was enough to make me step back a few paces, take a few deep breaths and centre myself.

The wounds looked to be around 4 days old, judging by the muscle wastage surrounding them and the level of infection. I didn't have the means or ability to save this creature, and I'm pragmatic enough to know that for my sake and the deer's, I needed to bite the figurative bullet and kill it. I could still save most of the carcass and pelt at this stage as the rotting tissue was fairly localised. The poor creature deserved an end to its misery.

It's safe to say that my wondrous mood had long since fled.

I unsheathed my Bowie knife and stepped around the other side of the deer. I stroked its shoulder experimentally to see if it would bolt. The creature didn't even turn its head to me again. At least this would be easy. I positioned my knife behind its ear and thrust it home. The deer shuddered all over and dropped like a stone.

I made quick work of gutting and skinning the poor animal, which being the local variety of mule deer would only have weighed around fifty kilos even at full weight. Between the dehydration and my own ministrations, I was only dragging thirty five kilos home, if that. I made a makeshift stretcher from a couple of long branches and my ever present roll of duct tape, and dragged him the mile or so home.

Once home I set myself to preserving the meat and tanning the hide. I have a decent set up here, racks for tanning and a smoker I built myself. This was the first deer I'd seen in years but there has been the odd furry critter put out of its misery over the years and it's time consuming to set up on the fly. Plus, I have the space. I also get bored... I actually have a lot of theoretically useful shit I barely use.

The meat served me well for a couple of months and that first night I had my first steak in a decade. I dropped it into the wood fire in my excitement to eat it and it burnt. It was the best thing I've ever eaten.

The leather and antlers on the other hand have given me two years of solid use. The hide I used to fashion myself the gloves, elbow, knee and arm pads, and the best fitting pair of boots you can imagine. (Made of duct tape and intricately sewn leather. They're the boss. Seriously.) The antlers went to some of my mods and a nice new handle for the Bowie knife. Seemed fitting.

The bulk of the antlers were formed into a spike of sorts, for lack of a better word. Each around one and a half centimetres at the base, narrowing to a sharp point. I treated these with my precious supply of super glue to harden them and used the same glue to attach them to several pieces of toughened leather reinforced with strands of tough bark. These I meticulously sewed into the fingerless gloves, elbow and knee pads. Which themselves required a great deal of meticulous sewing. And time. Like I said, I have it to spare.

With the force of a fist, elbow or knee behind them, my mods can punch a hole in your skull.

# **Chapter Two**

I secure each piece of my kit, checking every knot and strap with care, leaving only my boot mods, which I hang from my belt for the time being. These are great weapons, but they aren't conducive to running four miles as silently as possible. They are a sandal of sorts that secure over the heel and shin of the boot. This attaches a bark padded piece of fire and water hardened wood to my heels, giving my kicks bone shattering force, and bark padded toughened leather to my shins. Some of the bark around here is bitching.

I also pull on a similarly padded leather jerkin, which offers a little protection to my major organs. It's turned a blade and saved my life before, and sure does take the edge off a blow to the kidneys. Next is the snood and goggles and over these I slip the hood, made of the same materials, with extra reinforcement at the temples. I toughen and shape these pieces with the simplest of tools: water and temperature.

My machete, beautifully weighted, slides into its sheath on the back of the jerkin. My small hand axe is strapped to my hip and thigh. The Bowie knife lives permanently in its sheath on my right hip and two viciously sharp bone knives reside in my boots. I've also sewn hardened pieces of wood into the palms of my gloves and my arm pads. I feel like there's a name for those. Tracers? Brainers? It's not like I can just hop on The Google and check. Brainers is a good name. Apt. Let's go with that.

The sun has crept closer to the horizon, lending the sky a violently red hue as the light begins to flee. My eyes drink the colour in greedily. What an appropriate colour to light the last sky this filth will see.

Time to run.

I had intended to come across them in that grainy twilight, that no man's land between night and day when the sun no longer lights your surroundings, but dark hasn't set in quite enough for the customary fire to aid your eyes that much. Of course, I hadn't banked on that big of a fire. The last two nights they'd made a fairly standard sized campfire over which their slave woman roasted a dozen or so lizards and snakes and what looked to be some sort of root vegetable. There are ten men besides the woman. They all took their turn raping her after their dinner. She didn't put up a fight of course but there's no way she wanted that. I've come across gangs where the women run with and fuck them willingly, and participate in the brutality of their way of life. These women are still worth less than shit in the eyes of the men but they'll torture outsiders with the same fervent glee and offer themselves in exchange for the protection of their horde. If the men lose interest or come across a better specimen, willing or not, the woman/women will often be sacrificed to other needs. Everyone misses the taste of sweet, mammalian flesh and these men are not planning for the preservation of the human race.

This woman's hands are tied and her feet are hobbled every second that she isn't cooking, which tends to be a fair giveaway that she isn't there willingly. Or that they enjoy keeping her tied up.

I can see the glow of the fire from nearly two miles away this evening as I run, keeping a strong six minute mile. I can hear voices, some raised, some laughing, one sobbing as I draw closer. The rhythmic slapping of flesh becomes more apparent the further I run. The nightly satisfaction. I can smell the fire, the engines of the vehicles, even the rancid sweat of the men as I come to within a half mile of the camp, but I can't smell their dinner. Curious. There is small patch of trees to the east of their camp and I leave the road, such as it is, and circle around to the cover of the trees.

Working my way carefully and quietly through the woods, I keep part of my attention on the activity of my targets. Compassion for this woman would have me rushing in to rescue her immediately, or had me try to take them an earlier night, without a decent set of observations. While I hope for a good outcome for her, she is not my top priority. That would be my own survival, followed by the total annihilation of these men. Rushing in will likely ensure the demise of us both, and allow their continued bestial existence.

The assault is still ongoing. I can hear snatches of conversation now, hampered more by concentrating on my silent passage than by my hearing. I catch one guy crowing that they'd eat well tonight. I stop dead to listen, watching through the gaps in the trees as he lines up for his turn. He reaches over and twists a fist in her hair as he takes her and wrenches her up against him, turning her ear to his mouth. "Bet you wish you'd stayed laid down like a good dog now don't you? Dogs that run away or disobey get *put down.*" He takes her earlobe in his teeth and tears it clean off. She howls and her body jerks. He stuffs a wad of cloth deep in her mouth and shoves her face back in the dirt as he continues.

"No picking at it until it's done Flick. It has to go around 10 of us and I get the bigger fucking share, not you." The gigantic piss stain I'd identified as the leader plants a foot in Flick's back and shoves him forward, tipping him off balance. He lands on the woman with a meaty grunt, driving her body and face further into the dirt. I can't hear any noise at all from her. Flick mutters  under his breath that he likes it raw and continues with barely a break in this new position, hands on the back of her shoulders.

I keep moving after a moment. So she tried to run away and now they're going to eat her as punishment. Explains the giant fire. I catch sight of the fire on the other side of the group as I keep moving. It's about six feet wide and three feet deep, a proper pit dig out and lined with stones. They probably made her dig it out. They've been burning a vast amount of wood for a couple of hours and now it's a giant bed of incredibly hot smouldering chunks. I can feel the heat from here. They've set up a stand on each side and I see a blackened pole with L'Shaped ends about seven feet long. They plan to spit-roast her.

This is why I can't prioritise her wellbeing. Saving the future from brutes like this is more important.

The wooded area curves around the rear of their camp, bringing me closer to the fire, where their sole sentry sits. He has one eye on the festivities, one in the rough area of the vehicles, of which there are four. Two antique looking jeep type vehicles (I never did have much interest in cars), a truck with a large open flatbed, and a low slung, giant meathead car. You know, big engine, shitty handling and a license plate that might as well read 'compensating'. I'm guessing this is Piss Stain the Mighty's transportation. The jeeps and the truck have those cow stopper things on the front but his giant hulk of symbolism is unadorned. Not to mention less dusty.

I creep up behind the absentminded sentry, seated comfortably in one of those old school camping chairs, the folding kind. The main group are about ten meters away and the fire is in between. They'll struggle to see any commotion but silence is still key. I unsheathe one of my bone knives, take a moment to judge my shot, and in one swift motion take hold of his throat in a chokehold which cuts off his airway and thrust the blade into the space between his ear and jaw. I angle the blade upwards, straight through his brain. I smell the acrid stench as his bowels relieve and hold him still in his death throes. I position him to look as though he's simply nodded off. Nine standing.

I glance towards the vehicles, debating whether or not to disable them. I don't think my quarry are the type to run, not from one girl. Or small man. It's probably hard to be sure when I'm kitted out. I decide to forgo the time it will take. A quick glance tells me that the last man is lining up for his turn and they'll likely have someone come to trade with the sentry soon. They're democratic in their own disturbed way. I need to move.

I duckwalk to a shadowed area just in the trees, pulling out my blow gun and surveying the branches above me. Plenty of low slung sturdy branches. Perfect. I carefully slide in a dart, dipped in a combination of rattlesnake venom and belladonna juice. A potent elixir ensuring anyone hit by it will be delirious and crying for their mother within an hour, far less if hit near a major blood supply. The perfect way to hamper any runaways. I blow the dart at a man a few feet behind the man closest to me, striking him in the side of the neck. Pocketing the little tube, I grasp the branch closest to me and pull myself up into the tree. I leap through the branches of three trees spanning ten meters, setting myself carefully back down with the man still looking around him in bewilderment. He's trying to pull out the dart while shouting at the men behind him. He is having trouble - the ends are slightly barbed. Vicious little things that provide me great entertainment. The men are looking in different directions as the barbed man shoves the man directly behind him with one arm, the other still occupied with trying to pluck out the dart. His fingers slipping around in his own blood. I fire off another two darts in quick succession and pull myself back into the cover of the trees, slipping silently through the branches.

The men are troubled now, voices are raised. They are no longer used to feeling fear, if they ever were. They are turning away from the prone woman, though no one is looking in my direction yet as I have moved again from where I fired my darts. I am now directly facing the fire pit, with the men and the woman in between. Fire is an excellent weapon. There are around eight meters between my perch and the pit. Hanging from my belt are small balloons filled with clarified liquid fat. I throw two into the fire. The men miss the movement but they don't miss the fat exploding from the flames as the balloons burn through. The two men closest to the fire get showered. One goes up like a fireball. No helping him. Eight still standing. The other drops to the ground and rolls around, screeching and burning his hands beating at the flames. No one stops to help him. They all rabidly scan the darkness surrounding their camp, violence, fury and terror mingling with the sweat and dust on their faces.

The last man doing his business is still pumping away, seemingly oblivious to the chaos around him. It might be more accurate to say boy. He looks to be no more than fifteen, and people age fast in this harsh landscape. The Mighty Piss Stain realises this and turns to face the pair. He pulls the lad off and throws him on the ground, dick hanging out, covered in her blood. "Pay attention you little fucking prick!" he snarls, and drives his boot into the boy's face. Little fucking prick goes downtown. Not even a twitch. The burning ballsack has managed to put out the flames and is staggering to his feet, staring at fingers melted like candle wax.

Seven still standing. I can see the three I shot wobbling a little. The adrenaline and likely hunger are making my toxins work overtime. Time to dance.

After slipping on my boot mods I loosen one of the straps securing my trusty little axe and grasp hold of my machete. Piss Stain has his back to me and no one is looking my way. I run lightly on my tiptoes and separate his spine at the base of his neck with one swing of my machete, leaning back and planting a boot in the middle of his back, and thrusting his body forwards. He is propelled straight into Burnt Ballsack and returns him to the fiery pit he just escaped, his body holding Ballsack down in the flames. Five standing. I pivot and cleave the next man clean through the shoulder and sternum. He drops, taking the machete with him. I pull out my axe and throw it, ruining a man's throat and jaw. Pretty sure that was Flick. Three to go. The remaining three were all struck by darts. The violent exchange has lasted only a few seconds so far, and they are just turning themselves to face me. One, I am satisfied to see, has been struck in the eye and made a bit of a mess trying to pull it out. He trembles at the sight of me and drops to his knees. The powerful hallucinogens, the flickering quality of the light and my unusual head garb is no doubt resonating oddly in his addled brain. I kick him into the dirt and stomp on his temple with my wooden heels.

I unsheathe my lovely Bowie knife and survey the two remaining. Both unsteady on their feet, though the guy hit first has it worst. He looks ready to hurl. Yep. There he goes. I run at the next guy as he's distracted by his comrade tossing his cookies and jump with a raised knee, aiming high. I grab for his shoulders and use my momentum to take us down and we land with my spiked knee straight over his heart. He stares at me, eyes turning bloodshot instantly as he tries to draw a breath. I sheath the Bowie in his brain, by way of his mouth. One to go.

The original barbed boy is voiding every liquid in his digestive system, shaking on his hands and knees as spasms rack his body. Might as well be every liquid in his body. So I slit his throat and watch until he is still.

Done. I survey the campsite. I'm far past the point where gore bothers me but I still kill quickly and cleanly where possible. It's the smart way to play such a dangerous game. Don't be giving away chances for someone to return and fuck you up, and remember that others have survived this long because they're tough, if nothing else.

The woman catches my gaze. She hasn't moved an inch. I take a few strides and drop to a knee by her shoulder. She's still warm but there is a large stain beneath her hips. Probably a lot is blood but my nose tells me her bowels have emptied. This doesn't look promising. I turn her by the shoulder and roll her onto her back. No pulse. No breath. I rub some of the dust from her lips and see that they are blue and dark. I pull the cloth from her mouth. Her nostrils are clogged with dust, dirt and blood. She drew her last breath before Flick landed on her. I see the patch of blistered skin on her inner thigh, the permanent souvenir of surviving the plague.

I sit back on my heels, deflated. I had hoped that I could save her. I close her eyes, still wide and bulging in terror, and close mine for a few moments. I know I made the right decision in carrying out my plan before going to her aid, but I don't feel good about it in this moment. I open my eyes and allow them to drift over her ruined form. For the first time, I notice how distended her stomach is in comparison to the bones that jut from her hips and ribs. That belly button straining towards the sky. I drop my head into my hands and cry.

Once I gather myself I stand and look around, seeking a blanket or cloth to wrap this woman's body. I hear an odd bubbling sound, gurgling, guttural, almost rattling. I locate the source easily enough. Flick. Still breathing through the ruin of his throat. Jaw hanging to the side, tongue shredded and flopping around. His hands grasp at the place his face no longer lives. My grief and rage at the fate of the unnamed woman and her unborn child coalesces in my chest, becoming hard and bright, a diamond of pure, cruel fury.

I kneel in front of him, looking him in the eye. "Thought you like it raw, Flick?" He gurgles some more, blowing blood bubbles at me. I stand and drag him by his greasy dreads to the fire pit, which has already made good work of Piss Stain and Ballsack. I hold him over the deep layer of embers, allowing him to feel the heat on his raw nerves. Long enough for him to start to blister. Droplets of blood sizzle as they fall from him. "Well done it is," I murmur, before dropping him face first to his end.

I work quickly through the camp. As I expected, there is little of worth for me, excepting what the vehicles hold. A few guns, no bullets. Large knives, a few sets of knuckledusters. A bullwhip, clearly used freely on the woman, judging by its dull brown patina and the welts, both bloody and beginning to scar, crisscrossing her back, buttocks and flanks. I'm not interested in their substandard weapons. I move to the vehicles. I'll load up the truck with what I want and return home with it. To my delight, I find that the men have some sensible supplies after all. The truck bed is half filled with diesel canisters, all but a few full. Twenty in total. Wouldn't have lasted them much longer with these vehicles. I wonder if they had a destination in mind. I fill the empty ones by siphoning out the remnants from the other vehicles' tanks. They had supplies of duct tape, tough cord and rope, canned food, batteries, matches, salt, water purifying tablets, iodine and a healthy stash of painkillers and antibiotics. I load it all up, along with a couple of crowbars and hammers I found. And a few bottles of whisky. I find some thick fur blankets to wrap the woman up in Piss Stain's car and dig her a shallow grave. I leave the rest to rot after stripping their clothes and boots. Waste not if you live in a wasteland. They all have a patch of blistered skin, of varying sizes. The longer you took to fight it, the further it spread, until it could spread no further. I've yet to meet anyone without one, and the people I meet are always dead by the time I examine them, so I have time to check.

Except me.

I've opened the door to the truck's cab and am about to scramble up when I hear a low whimper. Almost a whine. I stop and listen. Hear it again. Coming from the back of the jeep I think? Could have sworn I checked it. I heft my (cleaned) machete and swing open the heavy back door. Just jumbled up blankets. I am turning away when I hear it again. A low, quivering whimper. I pull out the blankets one by one. My nose twitches. Urine? But...an oddly unfamiliar undertone to it. I pull out a clump and reveal a small furry...thing. A baby...dog? Is that it? What are they called again? Ah yes. Puppy! But largish for a baby. A child dog perhaps. It looks at me, all big ears and paws and eyes and fur. It cringes as I move my hand towards it. Poor puppy. Someone hurt you. It is a blackish brown with an auburn hint, long thick fur, big pointed ears, almost rectangular, tapered muzzle. I vaguely remember seeing a dog like this, before. I wonder where its mother is. Until I recall one of the blankets I used to shroud the woman. It was more of a pelt. Blackish brown with an auburn tinge. I gently stroke its head and neck, feeling it quiver and cringe. He or she will come to learn that I won't harm them given time. I cast my eyes downwards. Looks like a she.

Some part of my brain reminds me that my new companion will need a name. I rub the back of its neck thoughtfully. The only dogs name I remember is that of my beloved childhood dog. "I shall name you soon," I whisper to my new friend, as she gives my hand an experimental nuzzle.

*

There are those who might bandy the word, hypocrite, when describing me, for have no doubt, I too am violent. So much so that at times I question my own morality. I cannot argue that I kill in defense; though certainly it started that way. I got my first taste of the death I would inflict a mere month after the dust came, defending my family home, minus the family of course. For the next two years, until I was driven from there, I only killed in defense, in reaction, to protect myself, my home and my supplies. I had been a victim of violence my whole life - who was I to inflict that misery on others?

As well as this, back then, I had mercy. I will always recall the man, more a boy really, who had gotten strung up in one of my snares while approaching my land with his comrades. I dispatched his friends, a hard and bloody fight, and came across his swinging form while checking the land afterwards. He had been dangling by the ankle for many hours by the time I found him, and his face was so dark and swollen with his own blood that it took me a few minutes to realise how young he was. Fourteen perhaps. He had soiled himself and he reeked of the urine and excrement caught in his hair and clothes. I felt a strong surge of pity for this boy, so much so that when I cut him down, I ignored the instincts telling me to end his life now, and sent him on his way with a warning of death were he to ever approach my homestead again.

He never did approach my homestead again, but he and I would cross paths, over a year later, following my expulsion from home. In the early days before I set up my current camp, when each day was fraught with fear and uncertainty, sleeping in different places every night, in abandoned houses and trucks, or on the ground when I lacked options. With only my little bike and a few weapons to my name, hunting bow and arrow and a handful of knives, I scratched out an existence. I avoided confrontation at all costs, only killing when I could not escape.

But one night I was woken by a sound that clawed at my heart as I shivered in the lumpy bed I had chosen to slumber in that night. A child, a young child, screaming, howling, every note emitting pain, panic and pure, sheer terror. Stumbling to the window and peering out, to be met by a scene of such horror that even now after all of these years and all of this death, I have never seen anything to match it.

A pinioned and spreadeagled young woman, who thankfully seemed to already be dead, being violated with a knife by another woman, far older. Two men watching. Her naked breasts swinging like pendulums as she turned to pleasure them. The men continued to gaze at the brutalised young woman but my attention was caught by the now silent form of the child being rotated on a spit over the glowing fire, and the man, no, the *boy*, turning the spit. The same boy who in my stupid fucking *mercy*, I released to help commit this atrocity. I picked up my bow and for the first time, I killed from anger, from want, from *need, for **justice***, raining down arrows until only the woman remained, with my projectiles spearing her feet, preventing her from running from me.

As I exited the house I found her dragging herself backwards, away from me, leaving smeared bloody trails in the dust. I looked down at her, filled with a contempt I can barely even now describe and a sense of what was almost betrayal, that a woman could do this to another when womankind had already been so thoroughly *fucked over* by the events that came before. She appeared to me even less than human, barely an insect, the lowest of the low. She stopped trying to drag herself away and looked me straight in the eye, panting, lip curling, sweat coating her naked, time ravaged body like a greasy film. I could see it collecting in rivulets in every line, crack and crevasse in her weathered skin. She might have been thirty or fifty years old. She saw the question in my eyes before I even opened my mouth.

"This is the new world order girlie. Adapt or die." She smiled at me through the gaps in her teeth, but the smile didn't reach her eyes. I held her gaze until she dropped mine, dipping her head and glancing over at the woman, the first glimmers of shame on her face. She turned her head sharply from that scene, to be met with the child, still roasting over the fire, and decided it was better to meet my eyes after all. I could see the sheen of tears now, but found myself unmoved. "They'd have killed me if I hadn't done it! I didn't take no pleasure in it!"

When I sent an arrow through her eye, I most certainly took pleasure in it. Since that day, I've never passed up an opportunity to kill a killer, and I've never left a survivor in my wake. The alternative as I see it, is much worse.

# **Chapter Three**

It takes me two days to return to my home, in the base of the cliffs near a canyon in what was once a national park. I discovered this place many years ago, when I was driven from my childhood home. I collected my well hidden bike and rucksack along the way. The truck was well able to cope with the rough terrain leading home and the dog and I made excellent time.

In decades past I would never have been able to drive even close to this area. This was once a challenging hike of many miles. When Bogart Windross, (initially and amusingly given the moniker of Booger Farts) won the 2012 presidential election, he decided that the natural glories of America should be more accessible to those with wallets as big as their waistlines and spent a staggering amount of money on widening trails in various national parks so they would be accessible to off road vehicles. While of course completely scrapping Medicare, all welfare programs and state support, food stamps and state funded education. Who cares if children are dying of easily treated infections, starvation and diseases that were once eradicated by vaccines, so long as the wealthy can have great views of the canyons without breaking a sweat?

President Windross became Emperor Windross within the first eight years of his landslide victory, and America never saw another election. At the time the plague hit, The USATG (United State of America the Great, incorporating what were once known as Canada and Mexico) was ruled by Emperor Humphrey Windross. Bogart Jr and Carey Windross had both been publicly executed after Bogart Sr charged them with inciting insurrection ten years into his rule, and women, even Windross's precious daughters, had no real rights under his regime. When Windross passed in 2031 at the increasingly ripe age of 89, Humphrey Windross succeeded him, and ruled with an opulent, but iron fist. Until of course the plague claimed him in 2036, along with the majority of warm blooded life on the planet.

I have a great set up here, though it's taken years to build it up. I've made my home in a series of caves, close to the water but above the water line. I have my main cave and I utilise a few smaller nearby caves for storage. I roll back my camouflaging screens and set to stashing my new supplies, the dog watching me closely. I survey my stockpile with satisfaction when I am done. I was hardly short of supplies before this recent acquisition - I live off the land wherever possible, even if I have something in stock. It is safe to say that at least in my personal corner of the apocalypse, production has ceased.

I check my traps and am pleased to find them all filled with pissed off, soon to be deceased lizards. Seven in total and a couple of them look *meaty*. She eyes the woven cage I transfer them to with curiosity. I eye her with curiosity in return as I go about building my fire and setting up the spits. I have several of varying sizes.

I had worried about training her, as it's been so long since I've had contact with any sort of animal, let alone one with a domestic purpose. This dog though...I find myself wondering if she can actually understand me. She seems to pick up on my very thoughts. Our first night sleeping together after I rescued her I had been contemplating how best to secure her as I slept. I was reluctant to shut her in the truck given how quickly the temperature would rise with the morning sun and I was loathe to tie her with a rope in case she panicked and choked herself.

As I was debating what to do, she rose from her place by my side, trotted over to the truck and returned to me with a blanket clamped in her jaws. She dropped the blanket next to me, pulled the edges out and sat herself neatly in the middle. There she stayed, holding me steadily in her gaze. That curious, golden gaze. Her eyes were a deep, amber tinged gold, quite unlike anything I've seen on an animal before. She stayed firmly in place as I laid out my bedroll and built a small fire. I arranged my bedroll a few feet away from where she had laid out her blanket and turned my back to her to light the fire. I could hear fabric sliding softly over the ground and the light padding of her paws. I turned to see that she had positioned her blanket next to mine and seated herself in the middle again. She gazed at me calmly. Okay pooch. Point taken.

As soon as I had made up my mind to allow her to stay with me unsecured and my mind turned to the evening's meal, she rose to her feet and began sniffing and exploring the perimeter of our little campsite, staying in my sight at all times. She seemed particularly interested in one corner and after a few seconds of rapt attention she lunged forward. I heard a snap and a crunch and she returned to me with a sizeable lizard clamped between her jaws, twitching in its death throes. She dropped it at my feet and returned to her spot on the blanket.

We shared the lizard that night, along with the root vegetables I'd acquired from the raid the night before. She watched my every move, and I watched hers. She fascinated me. Part of it was the allure of having warm blooded company after so many years of solitude. I rarely allow myself to dwell on the harsher realities of my life. Maintaining a positive mental attitude is more crucial to my survival than any other aspect. But I have been lonely. So lonely.

I struggled for some time to identify the warm feeling that seemed to be growing in my chest as I laid down to sleep and felt her curl up next to me, nestling into my side. I felt her chest rising and falling, heard the breath entering and leaving her lungs. I could even feel the faint murmur of her heart beating against my ribs. I sunk my fingers into her thick fur and felt the warmth of her skin against mine. Is it affection that I was feeling? I think it may have been the first stirrings of love.

I breathed out, allowing myself to relax and identify the other emotion warring with the warm feeling in my chest. This feeling was less soft and warm, more bright and clear, with harder edges. Hope and fear. Two emotions that seem unable to exist without the other, for with hope inevitably comes disappointment, and I have not had reason to hope for as long as I can remember. And so, I named her for what she means to me.

"Goodnight Hope", I murmured, closing my eyes. I think I heard an answering yip in return as I slipped below the surface, smiling.

*

As the days turn into weeks and then months, I watch my new companion grow into the most beautiful animal I have ever been blessed to lay eyes on (though admittedly I might be biased). It takes her two months to grow to her full size, and that size is formidable. While it's been over ten years since I've seen a dog in the flesh and my memories may be flawed, I don't recall meeting many dogs whose heads could clear my shoulder. Standing on her hind legs, she towers over me.

Her fur is a rich motley of deep brown and auburn, with hints of bronze and gold. She seems wholly unaffected by the dust - I had worried about her eyes and respiratory system, but other than the pads of her paws, I never see or feel any dust on her. Those eyes, so deep and golden, can hold mine for hours, never needing to blink. From certain angles and in certain types of light, such as that of the setting sun, those eyes seem almost filmed, but not in a way that dilutes their clarity or depth.

Her claws and teeth are sharper than broken glass and her claws are serrated and retractable, another feature that I was certain didn't belong to canines. This made her approach almost silent. Despite her prodigious size and weight I can barely hear her coming, even with my incredibly sensitive hearing.

Hope spends a lot of time exploring the land in which I've made my home, and knowing that she will always return to me, I make no attempt to curtail these wanderings. I was wary the first few times she wandered off. The first two times she returned within the hour, but the third saw her leave me for three. My unease increased as the time wore on and as the sun marked the beginning of the fourth hour, I felt panic and fear flood my body, images of

Hope dead, eaten or stolen beating against my brain. I began scrambling to collect my weapons and gear, intending to track her and tear apart anyone or thing that might have hurt her. I strapped on my brainers and stopped short. Something was coming in my direction, *fast*. I could hear pounding, unusual footfalls, steady breathing, rustling leaves and snapping branches. I turned to face the approach, nocking an arrow and waiting.

Hope burst into the clearing around my home and put on the brakes. She was running so fast that she slid for a few meters before stopping, claws digging into the dust and dirt, leaving deep scores in her wake. I let out the breath that I hadn't realised I'd been holding and abruptly found myself sitting instead of standing. I tossed the bow to one side as Hope padded her way over to me and stopped in front of me. She had yet to reach her full growth, having only been with me three weeks at this time but already she was taller than I was when seated. She seemed to survey me for a moment, taking in my rapid breathing and air of panic. Hope leaned into me, lowering herself until her head was pressed against my chest. I felt myself begin to calm, my heart rate lowering. I leaned my head against hers and sunk my hands into her fur.

Did she feel my fear and panic? Did she somehow sense my worry for her? Certainly the timing and speed of her return would suggest so. I don't know exactly what I have on my hands here, but this is no ordinary dog.

I drew comfort from her closeness and once I was calm, Hope pulled back, resting her forehead against mine for a few seconds, before settling at my side instead. The message was quite clear. She will always come to me when I need her.

*

Since that day, Hope has regularly spent many hours a day running and exploring. Her speed is phenomenal. I took her with me on a scouting run when she was half grown and she easily kept pace with my usual speed of 20mph. I opened her up on a nice clear stretch and took the bike up to 40. Hope didn't seem to break a sweat.

One day I was practising my tree climbing and jumping skills, flying through the branches like a ninja monkey, or so I like to think. I cleared a 6 foot gap from one tree to the next and pulled up short. I hadn't been paying much attention to the sounds around me in the midst of my concentration and I became aware that I was being followed through the trees. I quickly scrambled up to the higher branches and perched there, utterly still and silent. A few seconds later, Hope burst through the foliage of the tree I had just leapt from and landed neatly on the branch I had just vacated. There she stopped and gazed up at me, her expression almost quizzical. She was using her claws to anchor herself to the branch, holding herself in a way that was distinctly feline. We had an abundance of cats when I was growing up, so I remember them well.

"So you climb trees too huh? Is there any end to your abilities, mystery pooch?" I didn't expect an answer of course. Hope continued to gaze at me, head slightly cocked to one side. I shook my head, confused, amused and undoubtedly impressed, and leapt for the next tree. Hope followed, somehow making less noise than me.

And so we trundled along, cohabiting so successfully as to be bordering on symbiotic. I made Hope a bed next to mine, padded like mine with bark, dried grass and a few furs I'd salvaged from my last hunt. Not her mother's pelt though. I buried that with the woman I'd failed. Hope would usually sleep here, next to me, and her presence never failed to give me comfort. Some nights though she would go off on one of her expeditions, and often at these times would not return until the morning sun made itself known. She always returned with food for me, to the extent that I felt the need to set up my traps less regularly. I dislike waste and while Hope will eagerly share my meals, she also has no difficulty sourcing her own food.

The more time that passed with Hope at my side, the more I began to notice changes in myself. I'd already observed improvements in my hearing and sight. My stamina and strength were already very impressive, given that I devote a large part of my day, every day, to various forms of physical training and conditioning. I began finding that the dust clung to me less and less, until I returned one day after a hard day climbing the local cliffs and found there was no dust to wipe. I considered whether the dust had simply decreased, but a casual glance at my outdoor equipment which I cleaned daily told me this was not the case. I gathered a handful and spread it over my forearm. The dust slid off as though my skin was oiled. My skin was...gleaming? Not quite shining. Definitely not sparkling. But there seemed to be a sheen, almost a glow to my skin that I haven't observed before. My skin feels curiously solid. Not hard, but as though there is less give to my outer shell. I'm usually covered in minute scratches and abrasions, a consequence of my love of hurtling through trees and scrambling up cliff faces, but I can't see a single mark marring my skin.

Interesting. Not that I have the slightest clue what these changes mean. My hearing and sight continue to improve and my standard, gruelling daily activities don't even cause me to break a sweat anymore. Hope's presence seems to have accelerated the changes that were already taking place in me.

# Chapter Four

I feel my father's weight settle on top of me. I smell his sweat, his putrid, alcohol laden breath. I feel his fingers pulling up my nightdress and tugging on my underwear. I whimper and struggle against him. "Please stop Father. Please." A massive blow impacts my jaw, stars explode behind my eyes and black flowers bloom from their centre, threatening to swallow me whole. I must stay conscious. I must stay alive.

Rough hands pinion mine above my head, both of my wrists held in a vice like grip by what feels like a giant's hand. Another hand clamps itself around my throbbing jaw and neck and twists my head roughly to the side. "I'm not your fucking Daddy little girl. Ain't no one to help you here."

My world comes rushing back. My father has been dead ten years. I'm in my cave and if the pressure on my neck and the rushing darkness is any clue, I might be about to meet my end. I pivot my hips, trying desperately to unseat my attacker, but I have no leverage. Strong and spry as I am, I am physically much smaller and lighter than this brute. My arms are pinioned in one of his, immobilising my upper body and his weight on my hips prevents me from twisting my body. I try to swing my legs towards me, try to hook them around his upper body but he swats me away as though swatting a fly and shifts his weight down so he sits on my upper thighs.

The darkness is intensifying and *I cannot breathe.* I desperately try to think with what sense remains to me. Hope! Where is Hope? She must be on one of her night-time expeditions. Or he killed her before getting to me. Even in the midst of my pain and fear, the thought of that causes another spike of grief and panic to lance through me. Focus! I twist my jaw sharply downwards and manage to sink my teeth into his flesh, clamping down with all of my strength. He swore colourfully and pulled his hand away, not reckoning that I would keep gripping with my teeth. A chunk of him stayed where it was and I feel the hot spray of his blood across my face and eyes. It stings. I wonder for a moment if he has any blood borne diseases. Not the time!

I drag in a lungfull of air, my lungs burning from the strain before another thundering blow comes crashing down. I cling desperately to consciousness, wriggling my whole body and thrashing in the hope of shifting this brute off before he succeeds in permanently subduing me. He rains blows on my face and neck and I feel my nose and cheekbone crack and give in to the pressure. My hands are still trapped in one of his and blood is pouring down my throat from my nose, choking me from the inside. His last blow catches me on my right temple, where the bone is so thin, and I can't keep the darkness at bay anymore. The fight goes out of me and the last thing I hear is his satisfied grunt and my bed creaking as he shifts his weight downwards.

*

Sunlight pierces my lids. All that registers is the pain and the brightness. I try to turn my face away from the probing rays, give myself some relief. I daren't open them yet. Pain lances through my neck and head and I stay the movement. I feel the sting as tears escape my eyes and slide down my cheeks. The literal rub of salt in my wounds. I hear movement to my left and the sun is momentarily blotted out. I freeze and try to open my eyes but they're gummed together and sealed shut. I let my other senses roam, trying to gather as much information as I can. The shadow shifts and the light pierces my eyes again, but it's much less painful this time. My eyes are adjusting.

First I take silent stock of my injuries. My face and neck are one heavy mass of pain. I can feel the skin over my cheeks and eyes straining, stretched to its limit by the swelling and bruising beneath. My nostrils are plugged, presumably by blood, and when I swallow I can taste the metallic tang in my mouth and throat. Speaking of which, swallowing is agony. I feel as though I've swallowed a red hot poker before trying to hang myself. I remember feeling my nose and cheekbone crack and being unable to draw breath for what felt like hours, so these injuries come as no surprise.

Moving down, I note that my hands are bound and I suspect my feet are too, though my feet are so numb that I can't be sure. I must have been laying on a very hard surface for some time. The ribs on my left side are on fire and my pelvis and thighs are throbbing. Between my legs...well I recognise that ache, that sting. The brute had his way. I can feel the stickiness where his seed smeared on my thighs. Judging by how sore I am, there's probably some blood in the mix too.

At this realisation, the fear that had been crowding my brain fled, to be replaced by a hard, crystallizing purpose. I'll rip his dick off and feed it to him before he bleeds to death. I've conquered dozens of men like this, but they've never encountered a woman like me before.

I listen now, letting my strongest sense tell me what it can. I can hear two men breathing, a fire crackling. Something metal being polished. One of the men sleeps, a few feet from the fire and around two meters from me on my right. The other I think is seated around three feet from me on my left. The sound of his breathing is coming from above as well as to my side. I hear his breathing alter slightly as he turns towards me and am able to approximate his location by the contrast he makes against the sun. I get the impression he is shaking his head as he turns his head back, and the sound of polishing resumes.

I smell the woodsmoke of the fire, the metallic tang of the polish, the fetid odour of the two men. I can easily separate the cheesy stink of their boots from the salty, pungent reek of their body odour. I can smell the grease in their hair and beards. I pick up on old meat and fresh liquor. These guys clearly don't have my hunting skills. My nose twitches. That smells like my whisky.

Now I'm really pissed. Distilling is a skill I've yet to perfect and I savour my occasional nightcaps.

*

The sun is rising and the day grows hotter. I feel the rays beating down on my bloodied face, drying the blood into a crusted, sticky mass, and reflect to myself that while I'm no doubt in mass amounts of pain from my various injuries, I'm otherwise faring better than I should be. My exposed skin should be burning, I should be sweating every last fluid from my body and my mouth should be as dry as the earth I lay on. But other than the pain, I feel remarkably well. My head is clear, my mouth is moist and I am as alert as I have ever been. The sun merely warms my skin, easing my soreness. So I lay still, feigning unconsciousness.

When the sun hits noon, my seated captor rises, staggering a little, a common side effect of necking half a litre of whisky. He stumbles over to the sleeping guy and shoves his shoulder with his foot.

"What the fuck man?" Comes the sleep slurred dulcet tones from the ground.

"Wake up Shit for Brains. Bomber and Spike haven't come back yet."

"Who gives a fuck man? They can do what they fucking want. I wanna fucking sleep, aight?"

"They said they were gonna load her shit up and get straight back here. It's a thirty minute drive from here. Spike was pretty insistent on leaving by mid-morning. You may recall the busted nose he gave you to drive the point home."

I hear a hawking nose and a splatter.

"Prick," Shit for Brains mutters. "I still don't see what the fucking problem is."

"The problem, Shit for Brains, is they should have been back hours ago. They've got the truck. So now we have to walk fucking miles to figure out what's happened to them. All the while carrying that battered bitch on our backs."

"Fuck that noise! I ain't doing shit to help that asshole!"

"You don't talk so big when he's around do you, little man? The reality is, we ain't got fuck all left in the way of supplies, they have the truck, and her supplies are eight miles west of us, since your dumb ass failed to return with  anything more than whiskey and her beaten ass. Do you want to wander on through what is a fucking desert half the time, with no supplies and no vehicle? Are you actually that fucking stupid?"

Shit for Brains jumps to his feet and leaps at the other man, who tosses him on his back with ease. I hear a squeal and a choked, gagging noise. I suspect the other guy has his boot against his throat. I risk trying to open my eyes a little. It's really, really painful but I manage to get the left eye open a slit. My suspicions were correct. A wiry, greasy man with matted dreads holds the aforementioned Shit for Brains down with his boot, and leans forward with his elbow on his knee.

"I'll repeat the question. You have one more chance to answer it. Are you actually that fucking stupid?"

Shit for Brains gurgles. The other guy raises his boot a fraction.

"N...no," he rasps, choking and gagging. "Sorry man."

The other guy spits in his face and releases him. Shit for Brains sits up, rubbing his throat and wiping his face.

The other guy looks my way and I close my eye, staying absolutely still.

"Why'd you have to fuck her face up so bad anyway? I like the colour of a bruise when I'm fucking a bitch but I don't like to feel like I'm fucking raw meat. Was the widdle girl too much for you to handle?"

Shit for Brains has the sense not to dive for other guy this time.

"She bit me man! Tore a chunk right outta me! I had to teach the bitch a lesson!"

"Yeah well taught man. If she wakes up to remember it. Either way, I'll take a quick turn before we head off. It's been months since we ate the last one and we might have to ditch her if we run into trouble. I'll turn her over, you managed not to bruise her ass too much."

Shit for Brains lapses into sullen silence as the other guy heads towards me. My pulse begins to race. I force myself to remain still and keep my breathing slow. He cannot know I am conscious yet. They will keep their worst tortures for when they think I can feel it, and right now there is no advantage I can wrest.

He grabs me by my bound hands, which are tied behind my back. My feet are definitely lashed together. I have on only a light tunic, now torn and bloodstained. No underwear, though I'd worn some to sleep. This movement causes pain to ripple through me, both from my injuries and from the unnatural angle and weight on my shoulders. I force myself to remain limp, hanging my head like a ragdoll.

The other guy throws me bodily over the chair he'd just vacated. The metal frame digs into my injured ribs and I can't hold in the hiss of pain. Luckily the sound of his boots scuffing the earth as positioned himself behind me covers it up.

Adrenaline spikes through me as I feel the movements of him freeing his dick. If I try to escape now, I will surely die. I'm nearly naked, my arms and legs are useless. I want to live. I have to let this happen.

The other guy spat on me twice and then on his hand to lubricate us. I feel him press against me and I can't breathe. Not again. I swore never again. Bile rises in my throat and I gag.

He laughs as he begins to thrust into me but stops short as a low growl seems to reverberate from all directions.

"What the fuck was that? You playing some kind of fucking joke Shit for Brains?" The other guy's voice is harsh and rough, angry but layered with an undercurrent of worry that I relish.

I risk opening my eyes. The other guy must have noticed me gag. He'll know I'm awake.

Shit for Brains is facing us, wide eyed with fear. I'm betting they haven't heard a sound like that for a very long time. I haven't either, but I'd bet my life, quite literally now I fear, that that sound was made by Hope.

The growl rumbles around us again, seeming magnified, surrounding us. The other guy could see Shit for Brains was not responsible. The other guy pulls away, dick now flaccid, likely from fear. He rises to his feet and tucks himself away.

"*Where is that coming from*?" he hisses, a genuine edge of fear and uncertainty to his voice. He pulls a gun from the holster on his hip. Looks like that's what he was polishing earlier. It gleams in the noonlight.

"It's coming from fucking everywhere man!" Shit for brains is frantically whipping his head around, wild eyed with fear.

"At least pull out your fucking piece, idiot!" Another growl rolls across us. It's so deep that I can feel it *in my bones*. Shit for Brains stares at the other guy, mouth open. Paralysed in fear and shock. I notice a widening stain around his crotch, and grin savagely. He took his pleasure from me. I will take mine from him.

The other guy notices the movement of my face and turns to me. He still looks sharp, though the hand that points the gun at me trembles.

"This is no time to fucking laugh bitch. I'll either put a bullet through your head or let you be eaten. Hopefully the first. That way I can still ra-"

Hope dives, seemingly from nowhere, and knocks the other guy away from me. She leaps straight for his throat and he throws his arms up, dropping the gun which rolls towards Shit for Brains, watching the unfolding scene with gormless terror. Hope tears at his forearms with her razor sharp teeth, her claws digging into his chest and legs. I see strings of flesh and muscle being stripped away and hear a sickening snap as her teeth shear through one of his bones with ease.

The other guy howls in pain and fury and screams at Shit for Brains, "Pick up the gun you fucking retard! PICK UP THE FUCKING GUN AND PUT THIS GODDAMNED BEAST DOWN!"

He takes a moment to register these words, and the other guy loses another bone. Then he dives for the gun, stumbling in his desperation and Hope turns on him snarling. Her muzzle and bright white teeth are dripping with blood and gore. Her eyes glow bright and golden. She is magnificent. I stare at her in awe, my pains momentarily forgotten. She is not just my hope. She is my saviour.

She opens her great jaws and envelopes his head in one bite, yanking her head away and ripping off his face and jaw in one movement. She tears into him with relish and the other guy somehow bolts to his feet and runs faster than I would have thought possible for a man with his injuries. Hope is deep in her bloodlust and in the few seconds she takes to look around, the man has disappeared into the canyon behind us. I look at Hope, willing her to stay with me. I feel desperately vulnerable.

Hope gazes in the direction the other guy ran for a few seconds and then pads softly towards me and lowers herself to the ground by my side. The lust seems to have passed and she sits calmly, waiting for me to move or speak. I doubt the other guy will be returning anytime soon, not with Hope present but I am nonetheless horribly vulnerable, exposed as I am. It's going to hurt, but I need my legs and arms to be free. I take a deep breath and roll myself off the chair. I have no control over this movement other than the direction I roll in, and the back of the chair is on my right, leaving me no choice but to roll to my left. I land heavily on my injured ribs and am momentarily swallowed by darkness.

When I come around, seconds or minutes later, Hope leans over me, gently nuzzling my face. If dogs can have expressions, hers would show concern. Thankfully I'm still on my side, since as soon as I raise my head to try and sit up, I vomit without warning. I lay still for a few minutes, breathing slowly through my mouth. When my world stops spinning I shuffle backwards a foot or so, worm style, to put some distance between myself and my meagre offering. I try to focus on my goal to distract myself from the fresh waves of pain that roll through me every time I move even a fraction. Each movement necessitates at least a few minutes of absolute stillness to be able to move again.

I have to give myself a stern talking to to muster the willpower for the next stage. I need to roll myself onto my back and bound arms, sit myself up and then scoot my hands under my ass and legs. Not the easiest move at the best of times let alone right now. One deep breath and I'm on my back. This brings a whole new breadth of discomfort and pain but at least my weight is off my ribs and I can breathe with more ease. I try sitting up using just my abdominal muscles, usually an easy feat for me, but my body rebels and just jerks off the ground and back again, flopping like a dying fish. I'm going to need some momentum.

I pull my knees up to my chest, momentarily crushing my poor hands as they take all of my weight beneath me and in one swift movement roll myself forward. I achieve verticality and lean forward into the motion, resting for a moment like this so that I don't flop straight back down. I then lean back onto my hands and put all my weight onto my palms, attempting to lift my hips and scoot my ass backwards through the gap in my arms. My strength fails and my hands lose purchase, slamming me back to the ground again. Black wings unfurl at the edges of my vision, like moths crowding into my line of sight, threatening to engulf me once more. I begin to cry, weakly, tiredly. I don't have the strength to keep myself upright while completing this manoeuvre. I could brace myself against the walls at the entrance to the canyon to give myself purchase and leverage, but they are around two hundred metres away from me, and they may as well be on the surface of the moon for how accessible they are to me in this moment.

After a few minutes of self pity, I roll myself upright again. There's nothing for it but to keep trying. This time though, as I lean forward, gathering my reserves, I feel a solid presence at my back. Hope is there. She lays herself behind me, pushing her body against my back and shoulders, providing me a platform against which to brace myself. To put her grown size into perspective, even laid down as she is, her shoulders and body easily match my seated shoulders in height. This time I am able to put most of my weight on to Hope, and use the strength of my legs to lift my hips. I shuffle my hands beneath my bare ass, and centimeter by centimeter, work my hands out from underneath me. Just as I feel like my shoulders will pop from the strain, the pressure eases and my hands are now bound in front of my pelvis, but still beneath my legs. The hardest part is over. I take a few minutes to rest again and then scoot my hands under my feet and over my knees. I lean back against Hope, panting harder than she probably ever has, and thank everything in the universe for her existence.

I look over at the faceless body of the man responsible for my current predicament and allow myself a moment of frustration that I was unable to mete out his promised punishment. Then I consider, while there are probably worse ways to go than having your skull degloved by a giant furious dog, I can't think of many. I'll take it. Shame about the other guy, though I can't imagine he's having much fun with his injuries either. He'll probably lose at least half of the injured arm and will likely die of infection along the way. I have bigger eggs to beat right now. Like cutting these damned ropes and dragging my injured ass home. Eight miles. Best not to dwell on that just yet. One step at a time.

I spy a sheath on the belt of the aptly named Shit for Brains, and shuffle awkwardly over to him to inspect its contents, managing to avoid the vile stain spreading beneath his pelvis. It's blunt, the blade is pitted and appears to be lashed to the handle with fucking twine, but it verily is a knife. I decide to free my feet first - the rope binding them is so tight I've yet to feel a thing from the ankle down. My feet are purple and swollen with a greyish tinge that worries me a little and the cord has dug deeply into my skin. I begin sawing where the rope passes over itself between my ankles, trying to keep the blade away from my skin. The blunt blade and my trembling hands aren't the best combination, and twice the knife slips and stabs my numb flesh. The skin doesn't break thankfully. I unwrap the severed cord, pulling it free from the grooves it has left in my ankles, and get to work on the bindings on my wrists, hoping to free my hands before the circulation and consequently, the pain, returns to my feet.

Freeing my hands proves much more difficult though, as I have no leverage to speak of and I am simultaneously gladdened and frustrated by the blunted blade. Frustrated that this is such painfully slow work, gladdened that I am not slicing fresh wounds in my fingers, palms and wrists every time the blade slips, which is often. A few minutes in, I'm barely a quarter of the way through the cord and the blood has begun to flood back into my feet, bringing with a sensation I can only describe as having a multitude of fire ants swarming under my skin. I drop the blade for the moment and massage my poor appendages, intensifying the fiery sensation but knowing that this will speed the process. The skin begins to lighten and grow pinker and less mottled, the greyish tinge fading. Hopefully there is no permanent damage.

I flex my feet and curl my toes as I return to the lashings on my wrists, repeating these movements as I continue to patiently saw through the bindings. As each cord in the rope parts, I feel more and more like myself again. It's been a long time since I've felt powerless.

"Thank you, Hope." I looked at my dearest, sat a few feet away from me, as the blade finally parted the rope tying my wrists together. I think she understands me. She has my gratitude either way. She moves towards me and I notice for the first time that she is favouring her left rear leg. I shuffle around to better see, not yet trusting my legs to hold me, and bade Hope to come lower, so I could take a better look.

There is a gaping slash just below her left hip, around six inches across and two inches deep. The wound seems fairly fresh – it has begun clotting but there is still some blood flowing. With the location of the wound, it's likely breaking open when Hope runs as well. I go over Hope's body, inch by inch, checking for other wounds, my own woes temporarily forgotten. She seems to have otherwise escaped unscathed and it's fairly likely, though not certain, that the asshat that bestowed the wound has already been summarily dispatched.

I scan the area, hoping to see something that might approximate some medical supplies. All I see are two battered rucksacks, presumably belonging to my abductors. Time to test my lower limbs. I rise gingerly to my feet with the aid of the chair. Hmm. Feels fine now. My feet have returned to their usual gold tinged creamy ivory colour and the indentations left by the rope have almost completely disappeared. The movement does make my ribs twinge in protest. Ok, maybe more than twinge. But I can move and hopefully run if needed.

I rifle through the rucksacks and come up short. All they have of use is a few canteens of water and they don't smell particularly fresh. Their clothing is filthy and greasy, their food old and looks to be spoiling. The one bottle of whiskey is empty by the chair the other guy was perched on. I'm loathe to bandage Hope's wound using the materials available to me. Hope is licking her wound as I search through the meagre items. In the bag that I suspect belongs to the other guy, with its cache of considerably better cared for weapons than the knife I plundered from Shit for Brain's corpse, I find a braided string, looped with small, suspiciously familiar white objects and scraps of what look like old, badly cured leather. I pull it from the bag and stretch it out in front of me. Yep. Ears and teeth. Had the other guy still belonged to society, it would have been a prison society. This has psycho serial killer stamped all over it.

Reluctant as I am to drink something I haven't sourced myself, I know I must need the water, so I drain one of the canteens and pour the contents of another into a tin bowl I found in one of the bags for Hope, taking stock of the situation. The other guy was right in estimating our location as being eight miles west of my home. I can usually run eight miles easily in an hour or less, without stopping to rest, but my ribs are going to hamper me today. I'm also barefoot of course, though this is less of an issue. I often run barefoot as a part of my conditioning and the soles of my feet are tougher than aged leather.

As it is, it takes us three hours to get home, Hope padding calmly at my side, never trying to run ahead. She seems barely hampered by her wound, while I experience a fresh bolt of pain to my ribs for every step that I take. I've made worse journeys I'm sure, but I can't bring them to mind at this moment. The trail of the truck is easy enough to see. I wonder why they took me so far before returning to my camp to loot it.

Despite my hardened feet I find myself limping by the time we have returned. I can smell the blood and effluence from over a mile away. Their truck is parked fairly close to the entrance of my main cave, and seems to be half loaded with some of my possessions. The camouflaging screens over my storage caves remain in place. Either they didn't notice that they were false or they had yet to explore that far. They certainly wouldn't make it now, since some important internal parts are spread really quite far from their bodies. What was left of their bodies. I sigh in resignation. While I am very grateful to Hope for dispatching these two, as well as Shit for Brains and the other guy, I could have done without the cleanup right now. I need to tend my own wounds as well as Hope's, dip into my stock of heavy painkillers and just shut down for a while. But the bodies are already bloated and stinking in this heat, though the accumulation of dust goes some way towards covering the festering wounds. The longer I leave this, the more of a nasty mess I'm going to ultimately have to deal with. I note as an aside to myself that there doesn't seem to be a single mote clinging to me, despite my long trudge and exposed skin, and my eyes though a little sore aren't all that irritated.

First things first, clothing. I feel immeasurably improved after donning my oldest and most patched pair of trousers and sliding my feet into a pair of looted, heavy boots. No sense in changing my torn and bloodied tunic until the messy stuff is out of the way or dirtying my better raiment. I pull my long blonde hair, currently matted with my own blood and crusted with dirt, back into quick pony to keep it out of the way, wincing as I unglue the numerous strands stuck to the blood coating my face. I thoroughly wash my face and hands and then wipe my hands and arms down with iodine, which I thankfully have a substantial stockpile of.

I select needle and thread, antibiotic cream, some bandages and a pipette and fill a bowl with clean water, before calling Hope to me and seating myself on my little stool next to her. She sits stoically while I examine the wound again. To my surprise, the gash is already beginning to pull together at the edges and it is fully clotted now. I fill my pipette and go to begin cleaning the wound when Hope pulls away from me. I stop, surprised, and beckon her closer to me again. She stands her ground, looking me in the eye for a few seconds before turning her head and licking at her wound again. I put down the pipette and pick up the antibiotic cream instead, dragging my stool closer to Hope with some effort. She moves away from me again, not far but just out of arm's reach. Gives me another level look and turns her head pointedly to lick the wound.

"Ok pooch. On your head be it." I'm not winning a tug of war with her and she doesn't have an issue with me looking at the wound, only with me treating it. Perhaps she knows something that I don't.

I empty their truck of my possessions – they'd loaded up part of my water stores and my charging solar batteries, and looked to have had my solar/battery powered water heater halfway to the truck. Thankfully all I need to do is push that back into place, which being essentially a giant copper vat, is not easy work, but at least they'd had the foresight to empty it first. I refill it and set it to start heating, so I can at least wash with warm water when I'm finished with the nasty work.

All told this took me an hour, and the sun is creeping lower. I don rubber gloves and an apron from my stash, take a deep breath, and start gathering the scattered entrails and body parts, depositing the disembodied remains in the now empty truck. The smell is vile and I have to run and throw up a few times, especially when I lift one of the corpses to place him in the truck and lose my grip. The corpse tilts downwards and oh boy, there were definitely some entrails remaining in this guy. I lose my cool at the feel of his slippery ropes sliding down my legs and bolt for the edge of my camp to hurl again. I hang my throbbing head, breathing carefully in and out through my mouth as I collect myself, then return to the task at hand. No point in lamenting something that has to happen. Best to just get the job done as quickly as possible.

When the bodies and various parts are loaded, I lift my bike into the cab with me and drive a few miles away, to the top of the canyon. I could just dump this anywhere, but I'm feeling the need for something a little more final. After taking my bike out, I reverse the truck right up to the canyon edge, leave it in reverse gear without setting the brake and hop out. There is already an incline and the truck would have gone on it's way without me, but I set my shoulder to the front grill and gave a good, solid shove to get it moving, regretting it instantly when my ribs howl in protest.

I ride back into my camp as the sun is setting and weariness settles on my shoulders like a weighted cloak. Still a few things to be done before I can crawl into my nest for the night. I strip off my soiled and stinking clothing and leave it in a pile at the edge of my encampment. I think I'll burn them tomorrow. The evening is still comfortably warm, so I stay unclothed as I turn to the task of examining my facial  injuries and settle myself in front of my old, spotted mirror. Hope is curled up napping when I return and raises her head to give me sleepy acknowledgment. Or at least, that's what I imagine she's doing.

Ooof. Yikes. Hmm. Well the other guy wasn't exaggerating much about the raw meat. My face blooms with the most fantastic range of colours. My left cheekbone bears some resemblance to a large plum that's swollen in the heat and been left to spoil. The skin has split over the most swollen point and the swelling appears to have pushed my left eye slightly out of place. I look as though I'm looking over my shoulder while also looking at myself in the mirror. I notice for the first time that my mouth feels different and open wide. Two teeth gone, on the left side of my jaw. I tongue the holes left in my jaw and don't feel any shards remaining. Hopefully they came out piecemeal. Dentistry is another art that is lost to me now.

My nose is canted to the right and like my cheekbone, is grotesquely swollen. This I can fix. I firmly snap the cartilage back into place, which is as painful as it sounds. Not much I can do about the rest except let it heal. My ribcage is black on my left side. I lay back and palpate the area, hissing with pain as I poke and prod, checking for anything that resembles a sharp edge. They may or may not be broken, but I can't feel anything protruding. I'll survive.

I drag my little bathtub over to the water heater and dump a dozen or so buckets of hot water into it, before lowering myself into the hot water, wincing at the sting between my thighs. I wash my hair and skin thoroughly, chew a handful of strong painkillers and chase them with a shot of my remaining whiskey, before crawling into bed. I spare a moment of my remaining consciousness to call out to Hope.

"Please don't leave me tonight," I murmur softly as she curls up on her bed, and for the first time this day, I embrace the rushing darkness.

# <u>Chapter Five</u>

*The other guy.*

*The sun beats down on his head as he stumbles along the canyon bed. The high sides of the canyon will offer protection from the sun shortly, but for the next hour, he must suffer. He cradles his ruined arm to his chest, dripping blood as he goes, the foremost thought in his mind to avoid leaving a trail for the hellbeast that tore him and Shit for Brains apart. So he stumbles and splashes through the slow moving water, slipping and tripping over rocks and detritus, hoping the running water will be enough to disguise his scent, which even he will admit, is prodigious. Add to that his dripping trail of blood, and he is not feeling that hopeful.*

*He bleeds less than you might think, given the extent of his wound, and one can only assume that no arteries were shredded during the attack. The man seems remarkably resilient, even with this as a factor. When the sun slides over the top of the canyon, granting cooler shade to the injured man, he allows himself pause to take stock of his situation.*

*He had expected the hellbeast to be on him by now. He's never seen anything that large and fast, even before the mammals and birds all but disappeared. That thing was larger than the largest wolf, and he would know. His occupation before the plague was poaching animals for their fur, pelts and meat, and he'd killed a few wolves in his time. Like many of the men who survived the plague and the resultant massacres, he had also been a killer of men and women long before the plague allowed him to do so with impunity.*

*If it hadn't found him yet, perhaps it wasn't looking for him. Which opened a whole new train of thought. He had assumed that the beast was a wild creature, the attack random, and that the slut would have been dispatched along with Shit for Brains. Now he remembers her smile when Shit for Brains pissed himself, the utter lack of fear when he pointed the gun between her eyes. Those eyes that not only lacked fear, but glinted with triumph. How the attack launched when he made a direct threat to her life. The other guy hunted with the aid of dogs in times past and knew first-hand the loyalty of dogs. He concludes that there is a strong chance that the dog is hers, and if so, they have likely left the scene to return to her nest in the cliff base. He has no supplies to speak of, and little hope of attaining more in his current state. This however is not a man who can recognise defeat, and unlike the majority of his peers, is not unintelligent.*

*He turns back the way he came. If he returns to the site and the slut's body is not there, his suspicions will be confirmed. So he trudges back through the canyon, walking on dry ground now that the need for undetected escape seems to have passed. He makes good time even without his prior urgency, since he's not constantly stumbling and slipping on wet rocks. He pauses when he reaches the mouth through which he entered the canyon, and peers in the direction of the rough camp that he fled. He sees no movement and can only make out one body huddled on the ground. He feels safe enough to approach, scanning his surroundings warily as he goes, alert for any sign of movement. But there is none, and he reaches the site without challenge or incident.*

*He takes in the scene, gazing dispassionately at the remains of his one-time ally. Not much of a loss as far as he was concerned. He doesn't object to his actions, merely his stupidity. Who raids a well-equipped camp like that and returns with only whisky and a body to fuck? The way he described it, she had enough in the way of supplies to last them a year. He can see the disturbed earth and dust where the slut rolled herself off the chair and presumably freed herself. He notes the small pile of vomit and enjoys a ripple of pleasure as he remembers the sensation of sliding into her unwilling body. He smiles, recalling the convulsion that seized her when he forced entry. This is a man who has always preferred rape to consensual sex. This is a man who not only enjoys the pain of others, he actively seeks to inflict it. This is not a man who believes in the concept of 'live and let live'.*

*He observes the sawn, frayed ropes, the two rucksacks, the contents dumped carelessly on the ground. She seems only to have taken the water canteens, leaving his cache of weapons, his binoculars and small, spoiling stash of food. He has little else of note, a few lighters, a small can of lighter fluid, (his last), a few scraps of fabric he uses to polish his weapons, torn from the clothing of his victims. She took the time to throw his trophies in the fire. His growing anger sharpens at the realisation, hardening into hatred. He hates this woman, this slut, this **whore** who has defied him and lives to tell the tale. This is not a man who is used to being challenged by those he considers beneath him. This is a man who takes what he wants, and enjoys using force to take it. This is a man who takes vengeance.    There is a chance, albeit a slim one, that the beast did not return with the whore, or that the beast has strayed again, as it must have when Shit for Brains stumbled into her camp. His next step, he concludes, must be to assess her situation, and see if any advantage can be wrested from it. He considers his left arm, which he cradles to his chest. Both bones in his forearm are snapped, which he knows as he can quite clearly see them. The layers of skin, fat and muscle have been torn away, and his remaining flesh hangs in strips. If he pokes around the flesh still on his forearm, he can see his veins pulsing and throbbing. His hand is ironically quite intact, but equally quite useless, as he cannot move a single finger. It would be generous to say he knows little about medical treatment, or even first aid. He knows enough to see that even with the right knowledge, his arm probably cannot be saved. Still, he must try. He has seen the application of splints before, and manages to source a fairly straight, rigid stick. He divests his deceased comrade of his shoelaces and hunts through his pile of pathetic belongings, finding a shirt. It's filthy, like the rest of Shit for Brains and his possessions, but his options are limited. He uses the shirt to bandage the gaping wounds, then places the splint and ties it in place with the shoelaces.*

*He returns to the canyon to drink until his belly is full, having neither the appetite nor the inclination to eat the spoiling food, and points himself west. He remembers the route to return to* their last campsite, and Shit for Brains had described the route to her camp from there. He sets off with the sun in his eyes, a sensation which doesn't bother him, and follows the whore home, his steps only hours behind hers.

He walks the first six miles with little care, following the tracks made by the returning truck when they curved away from the route that would have led to his group's prior campsite. He comes to a fork, one branch of which judging by the tracks will lead him to her camp, the other seems to lead to the top of the canyon a few miles away. Shit for Brains said her home was in the base of the cliffs on the opposing side of the canyon. Well he said her home was in the base of some cliffs. The other guy was able to follow the majority of the other road with his eyes as it wound upwards and figured that that was the case. The whore seemed mildly intelligent at least. She would have close access to freshwater without risking flooding in the winter, and her choice of location would be difficult to stumble across. Shit for Brains only came across it by chance when hunting.

He stood for a few minutes, lost in thought, when he became suddenly aware of the sound of an engine approaching. A familiar sounding engine. He dived off the rough road into the bushes and shrubs, screening himself from view and crouched low, watching as the whore drove past in his fucking truck. She took the fork that seemed to lead to the top of the canyon and gunned the engine, blowing thick clouds of dust into his face and eyes. He coughed a little, wiping the dust from his face, though the dust didn't seem to bother him as much these days, and had never bothered him to the extent it had his transient comrades. He hadn't spotted the hellbeast sat beside her in the cab of the truck.

He doubts a beast that size could be easily hidden in the cab of that truck, and why would it be hidden anyway? He risks creeping along a little further, keeping now to the sides of the roads, as hidden as possible, and pulls out his binoculars. He scans the horizon every few minutes, awkwardly fumbling the binoculars with his single working hand, until he reaches a vantage point where he is hidden, but has some view of the camp. He reminds *himself to be as quiet as possible. The beast undoubtedly has far better hearing than him, though he's noticed a definite improvement in that area of late. He sees the beast curled up near a large opening in the cliffs. Its size, even from this distance, is astounding. He had wondered if fear had magnified his memory of the beast. He positions himself as comfortably as he is able, and settles in to watch.*

*A few minutes later, he hears an almighty thundering crash in the distance, followed by the sound of a much quieter engine returning. He assumes the truck is no longer of this world. He watches as the whore returns to her cave dwelling on a small, off-road style motorbike, and continues watching with a curious mixture of lust, hatred, fury and even a touch of shame, as she strips, tends to her wounds and washes herself. Not shame from watching her ministrations, or shame of the lust that stiffens his cock even through the excruciating pain. He feels shame that he was bested, that he didn't take something that he wanted, at least not fully. He promises himself that he will have her, all of her, and break her. He promises himself that she will beg for the death he will give her.*

*She calls to the beast, which follows her as she retires to the depths of the cave. 'Hope', she calls it. He considers that a misnomer.*

*He watches through most of the long night, thinking, musing, considering and discarding possibilities for revenge. There is no movement from the cave, but he dare not approach, not with the beast inside. How can he reach her with the beast ever present? Ridding himself of it is surely the key to any plan.*

*The other guy rises to his feet and melts into the darkness.*

# Chapter Six

"Ayla. Ayla. Wake up please. Ayla. Ayla!"

I am jolted from my slumber at the sensation of a small hand pulling at mine, pulling with urgency. I register the fear and urgency before I register who is pulling at me and bolt upright in bed. I hear a thud and a clatter and open my eyes to the sight of Tilly, my sweet Tilly, sitting amongst the detritus of my cluttered nightstand. "You scared me and I fell." Her lower lip trembled and her wide eyes brimmed with tears as she stared up at me from the floor.

I scooped her into my arms, cradling her tiny, three year old's body against mine and kissing away her tears. Love for her surges through me, as it does every time I see and hold her, and reflect for the thousandth time that she will never understand the true depth of my love for her. I deposit a final kiss on the crown of her sweet smelling head and tuck her soft blonde hair behind her ears.

"What's troubling my silly Tilly? What can Ayla do to make you happy again?" I asked, tickling her little chin. Usually this gets me a smile at the very least but today she just turns those luminous, wet blue eyes on me.

"Mummy and Daddy won't wake up."

That's when I register that the light is wrong. Well, wrong for my usual Autumnal wake up time anyway. Usually Mother is gently shaking me awake at five am to help her with the animals, lighting the fires, making breakfast, the usual morning chores. Father usually stomps out of bed around ten to begin his work of collecting online conspiracy theories and speaking to my mother and I like we're no better than the stray dogs that he hurls his empty beer cans at from time to time. His father left him a decent sum of money and this small farm when he died. Father planned to live off that and we could either live off the land or die of scurvy for all he cared. The appalling laws of human rights under which we've lived over the past two decades gives Father the right to not only bar our access to work and education, but to neglect to provide for us, abuse us - even kill us, and face no legal consequence.

The light streaming through my window makes me think it's mid morning, and when I dig my clock out from amongst the detritus now on my floor, I see I'm correct. It's 9.35, and I've never known my mother to sleep so late.

"Ayla I'm hungy." The despondent little voice reached my ears again.

"Alright little miss, I'll get you some chow and then I'll check on mummy and daddy, OK?"

I don't think much of it as I scoop Tilly up and head to the kitchen. She's far too scared of our Father to make much noise trying to wake them, so I assume my Mother has just overslept and Father hasn't woken up yet.

I scramble her some eggs on toast, heat a cup of milk and deposit her at the kitchen table to eat. I should have just enough time to rouse Mother before Father wakes and gives her hell for oversleeping.

I poke my head around the door to their bedroom. The curtains are drawn and the room is dark and stuffy. There is an odour I can't identify, sweet, cloying and thick, almost suffocating. I can make out my parents, both lying still beneath their bedding. I softly move to Mother, and give her shoulder a little shake. No response. I shake her shoulder harder and whisper her name. No response.

"Mother? Mother?" I shake her again and pull the covers down a little. This time I hear a low groan from her, but no movement. I'm speaking full volume now and I hear nothing from Father either. I open the curtains, *open a window*, cause holy hell I'm about to choke on the air in here it's so thick. Neither of my parents even twitch, though Mother gives another low groan. Sweat lies thick on them both, casting a glossy yet milky sheen on their features. Their cheeks are flushed an unhealthy, almost tomato red. Their lips are crusted and their mouths look almost chalky.

I pull the bedclothes off Mother and see that her entire left arm up to the shoulder is covered in what looks like blistered skin, red raw and weeping. I pull her nightgown gently to the side and see that it extends over her breasts and down the left side of her abdomen too. I've never seen anything like this. The...rash? Affliction? Reaches as far as her collarbone. The sight of that dry, chalky mouth and the odd, milky sweat make my stomach clench, and coupled with the sweet yet repulsive scent, it's all I can do to not hurl over them both.

A perfunctory glance tells me Father has the same affliction. I try to rouse Mother to take some water, but all I elicit is that awful groan. I moisten a rag and trickle water into her mouth. It simply leaks back out and dries on her cheeks. By now Tilly will have finished her breakfast and will be getting curious. I stroll back to the kitchen, closing their bedroom door behind me.

"Hey there little miss, mummy and daddy are feeling a bit sick today so they're gonna stay in bed. That means you get to do fun stuff all day, and Ayla will help you choose and help you if you need me, but Ayla needs to look after mummy and daddy too. Is that ok my Tilly Lilly?"

Tilly gives this some thought, and nods solemnly. "Can I help mummy and daddy too?"

"Not today sweetie. Today I want Tilly to have lots of fun and make lots of noise, OK?

"Noise?" Tilly's eyes widen. Loud noise and raucous play were heavily discouraged in this household, unless it was Father ranting and raving.

"Yes! All the noise you like, deal?"

"Deal!" those wide eyes gaze up at me, shining with happiness, and I try to quell the wave of unease rolling through me so that she doesn't see it and get worried. She's a highly perceptive and anxious little thing, not surprising given the reality she lives in, and I don't want to cause a panic attack.

I direct her to the living room and pull out her blocks and homemade dolls, and tell her to call me if she needs me, not to come and find me. She nods absentmindedly, already adrift in a dream made of a whole day of playtime. She won't actually make much noise out of habit, but thinking she can will help her relax.

I return to the bedroom, bracing myself against the smell and go straight to Mother, picking up the rag to try again with the water. Has her rash extended further? I could have sworn it was just touching the collarbone before. Now it extends over it. Surely nothing moves that fast? I step back now, afraid to touch them more. I have no idea what this is and if I'm right and not just imagining it, it's spreading fast.

I return to the lounge where Tilly is happily building a castle for her dolls, and find a black marker. I use this to mark the edge of the rash on Mother's collarbone. I'll check it again shortly and see if it has spread.

I'm way out of my depth here. I have no idea what this might be, I have no idea how dangerous or contagious this is and I'm all alone, sixteen years old and needing to care for Tilly. We have no neighbours, at least not for many miles. There is only one phone in the house and it's kept locked in Father's study, along with the keys to the family truck and Father's old solar converted scrambler bike. The sole television and computer are also kept in there. Father doesn't see the need for us to have access to these things, since our only purpose is to care for him and our potential future husbands. I don't know if other fathers are the same. I've never had any meaningful contact with the outside world, beyond a short hospital stay three years ago.

Father keeps the keys to the study on his person when he's not in there during the day. I have to assume the keys will be in the bedroom with him. I rifle through the pockets of his clothes, piled next to his side of the bed in disarray and come up short. I check the drawers on his side of the bed. Nothing apart from his revolver. I sigh and eye my father's limp, sweaty body under the covers. The idea of touching him is revolting to me. I pull back the blankets. He lays prone, wearing sweat stained underwear and a vest top. His belly bulges, straining the fabric to its limits, his paunch hanging over the waistband of his underwear. I can't see any pockets, but I spy a cord around his neck, disappearing beneath his vest top. I follow the outline of the cord and spy the key tucked just below his right armpit. I give the cord a tug. Father gives his first noise of the day, a low, almost animalistic groan. The key doesn't budge. I pull on the cord again, with a little more force. He moans again, louder this time, and his leg twitches. The key is not forthcoming.

I grit my teeth and lift his undershirt, or at least I try to. The fabric lifts a few inches but then halts as though stuck. I give it another pull and some of his skin seems to lift away at the same time. He lets out another moan and I keep working on peeling back the shirt, ignoring the sounds emanating from him as more and more of his skin comes away. I have to get to that key. The shirt is almost completely melded to his rash. I finally expose the key and see that it's deeply embedded in the oozing, angry skin below his armpit. I take a deep breath and pull hard on the key. It finally pulls free from its fleshy prison, strings of what look like melted skin extending from the key to the hole it has left in his side. He lets out an almighty bellow and I leap back in fright, stumbling as my foot catches in his clothes –

I bolt upright, heart hammering, gasping and gulping for breath. My mouth is dry in a way that it never was yesterday and I gulp frantically from the water bottle beside my bed. Hope has roused herself and is staring at me with her head cocked, clearly aware of my distress but confused as to its source. I don't know how I know that, I just do. I may not be able to read her mind, but I seem to get feelings that are not my own when she is around, and they must be emanating from her. I've long suspected that Hope can sense my feelings too.

It was very hard to pick apart the roiling mess of emotions we went through yesterday, but I kept getting wafts of sorrow and…shame. As though she felt she had let me down. I don't know what delayed Hope in reaching me yesterday. Several hours had clearly passed between my abduction and her rescue, and we weren't separated by enough distance to account for that. Her wound didn't seem to slow her significantly. Perhaps she had strayed far enough during the night to have not felt my terror when I was attacked. Perhaps she was sleeping at the time. I'll never know, but the last thing I feel is disappointment or anger. Late or not, she saved my life yesterday.

As my heart rate slows and I begin to calm, the dream receding, I feel other emotions that aren't my own. A certain…resolution? A protective sense of determination. Hope meets my eyes and I know, with absolute certainty, that she will never willingly leave my side again.

My face seems to have some sort of slimy residue on it. I wipe at my face and the moment is reminiscent of sponging milky sweat from my mother's forehead. I shake my head to clear it. I glance over at Hope and get a waft of…satisfaction. As though something has worked as planned. Confused, I look from my now slimy hands to her face again, and she trots over and licks my face. With a clear sense of an action repeated. So it is Hope's drool shining up my face. Cheers pooch.

Shaking my head ruefully I motion her over so I can check her wound. Her movement seems unhampered today. I stare at her in awe. Her wound looks *weeks* old. It has knitted together fully, there is no leaking pus, puffiness, or redness around the wound. I lean back, meeting her eyes. If a dog could look smug, she does.

I pad over to the mirror on bare feet, to examine my own injuries, and am met with the sight of my own shocked face. I haven't made the kind of miraculous progress Hope has, but I'm looking infinitely better than I should be. I should be looking worse than I did yesterday. Deep bruising, tissue and bone trauma can take days to develop fully on the surface skin. I however, look as though I have had several days to heal. The swelling has almost completely reduced and my eye is looking dead centre again. Some of the bruising has already turned green and yellow and my nose looks to be healing straight. My ribs are a mottled mix of purples, blues and greens. The pattern is almost pretty.

The wave of smugness rolls over me again, and I turn to look at Hope. "So. Either your saliva has super magic healing properties, or your licking and proximity to me have enhanced the changes that were already occurring. Or both." Hope continued to gaze at me, but I got nothing in the way of a response. I'm not sure what I expected.

It's hardly a cause for complaint. I chuckle and turn to making myself a meal of berries, nuts and dried lizard meat, while Hope rustles around in some nearby bushes to find her own. She stops short at the edge of the clearing nearest the road, circles a spot on the ground a few times, and then *growls*. I feel it vibrate in my bones, feel her suspicion in my chest. I walk to her as quickly as my ribs will allow and see her attention is fixed on a dead lizard on the ground. I'm not in the habit of eating anything not killed by Hope or myself. I go to pick it up to toss it further into the bushes but Hope growls again and I stop and look at her. She nudges my hands away from the lizard and barks at it. She is not afraid but she wants me to understand this is dangerous. I hurry to the cave and back, returning with a small but powerful flashlight to better examine the lizard, as it is in the shade, and rubber gloves. Hope lets me examine it now and I see this lizard was killed by a knife and then the wound was scored. To make it look as though it was bitten perhaps. To eyes less keen than mine now are, perhaps that is in fact what one might see. Something has been smeared around the wound, mixing with the blood. A filmy, almost invisible layer. I sniff it. Belladonna.

I rise to my feet and after a few seconds, decide to burn the carcass to prevent other wildlife from ingesting it. The discovery sours my mood, which had lifted considerably.

It's not that I'm overly worried. I trust that Hope will not leave me, and I trust that no men will reach me when she is by my side. I know that Hope is too clever to be caught by such a trick. But knowing that someone, maybe the other guy, is trying to hurt me, hurt *us,* when I'm still hurting so badly from yesterday, is disheartening and I burn the carcass and knock back some painkillers with a troubled mind. It must be the other guy, or one of his crew, maybe someone who escaped. I feel Hope wanting my attention and turn to her. She wants to track. She wants to follow.

But I can't follow her while she does so. I can't bear the thought of being without her right now. Just the thought of her leaving causes panic to swell in my chest, adrenaline spiking through me, my mouth dry as a bone. She runs to me and presses that great head against my chest. She's not going to leave me. I breathe more slowly and gather myself. I'm feeling exhausted, though I've only been awake a few hours. I find myself swaying a little where I stand. Hope nudges me backwards and I stumble in the direction of my bed, curling up and laying my head down as Hope sits in the cave entrance, alert and awake. I idly watch the sun gleaming off the golden tones in her fur and then I'm -

Falling backwards and colliding with my parent's bedroom wall, heart hammering with fear and adrenaline. But Father doesn't wake. He lets out that subhuman bellow and his body shudders all over, but he remains unconscious. Clutching the cord with the key I scramble backwards out of the room, like a startled crab. I close the door and lean against it, trying to breathe more calmly, when Tilly comes running out of the lounge, her face tight and white with fear. "It's ok sweetie, Daddy just had a nightmare and fell out of bed. Everything is ok now." I palm the key so she doesn't see it, ignoring how slippery it feels against my skin.

Tilly studies my face in that haunting way of hers, trying to figure out what I am feeling. I'm sure I also did this at her age. You try to work out what people are feeling before you approach them in a household where you might get battered, or worse, for saying something at the wrong time. My poor Tilly already has scars, thin stripes where our father has whipped her across the legs and back. The scars he gave me when I intervened are worse, but it took his attention away from her.

"Then why you look scared too Ayla?" her voice trembles but even in her fear she wants to know I am ok.

"Daddy just gave me a fright when he shouted is all, like Ayla accidentally gave Tilly a fright this morning."

Tilly accepts this and turns back to the lounge, though she casts a final, worried glance over her shoulder at me. I smile at her, and wait for her to shut the door behind her before heading to the study door and unlocking it quietly. I go straight to the phone and dial 911. Though I'm not allowed to use the phone, my mother instructed me on how to use one in case of an emergency. The phone rings, again and again, seemingly without end. Is it supposed to do that? Shouldn't someone pick up? Isn't this the emergency line? I turn on the television while I wait for someone to answer. It automatically turns to a channel that seems to show news.

The screen is dominated by a silver haired man with dark, worried eyes. He is telling me not to panic, that there will be answers soon. Beneath him runs a banner repeating the same message, over and over. Stay indoors. If you or a member of your family are infected, do not go to the hospital. Do not go to a doctor. Stay indoors. If you or a member of your family are infected, do not go to the hospital. Do not go to a doctor. Stay indoors.

The silver man tells me that over the past forty eight hours, an estimated forty percent of the population of The United State of America the Great have reported symptoms of what has been provisionally named 'Bubble Flu', named so because of the bubbling, melting appearance of the accompanying rash. He tells me that the flu is either highly contagious, or is transmitted by unknown organisms in the air. The Empire's best minds are working on identifying the source and the cure as we speak.

He tells me that all hospitals have been closed to prevent further contamination. He begins to tell me that there have been reports of some animals being affected by the flu, when he stops and touches his ear, leaning his head slightly to the side. The banners beneath him stop rolling and begin flashing the same two words. ***Breaking news…..Breaking news…..Breaking news…..***

The silver haired man looks directly into the camera. "It is with the heaviest heart that I now must tell the world, that Emperor Humphrey Windross Jr and his family have all been infected with the Bubble flu. We are also receiving reports of high ranking government officials and royalty from Europe, Africa and Asia being infected. The Centre for Disease Control and the World Health Organisation have officially designated this event a global pandemic."

The silver haired man looks away from the camera, unconsciously touching his ear again. I notice a sheen across his forehead. Is that sweat from the stress he's under or does it have a milky sheen, like my parents'?

"I am now receiving reports of the first deaths officially attributed to the Bubble Flu. A hospital ward for the elderly in Minnesota, where the first cases of Bubble Flu were reported, have indicated that eight of their ten initial patients have died. The cause of death is preliminarily thought to be respiratory failure."

He pauses and touches his ear again. It occurs to me that someone is feeding him this information and he is reacting to it while sharing it with me, and possibly the entire world.

"We will have Dr Johnson from the CDC joining us live in thirty minutes to share with us his findings and recommendations." He pauses and looks directly into the camera again.

"In the absence of Emperor Windross, the Surgeon General and the Commanding General of the USATG Army, have declared a state of quarantine. They have further declared that martial law is now in place. Do not leave your homes and property. Do not make contact with friends, family or neighbours outside of your direct household. If a member of your household is infected, it is recommended that they are quarantined in a separate area, and that no further contact is made with them. We will return in twenty nine minutes with Dr Johnson, who has some information to share with us. Be safe."

I can see the silver haired man cast his eyes downwards, see his shoulders slump and his face crumple, before the camera cuts from him to a screen with a dark background rolling the same message on repeat.

"The USATG is now subject to martial and quarantine law. Do not leave your home. Do not make contact with others. Quarantine your sick and your dead. Do not infect your neighbour. The USATG is now subject to martial and quarantine law. Do not leave your home. Do not make contact with others. Quarantine your sick and your dead. Do not infect your neighbour."

I stare at the message repeating on screen. I know my mouth is hanging open but I can't seem to move a muscle. I attempt to turn the television off and realise my hand is empty. Hands. The remote and the phone are both on the floor. I must have dropped them. I don't remember. I pick them up and turn off the television. I'll turn it back on for the scientist's broadcast, but I don't want Tilly to see or hear any of this, not yet. Not ever if I can help it. I raise the phone to my ear, but it's not longer ringing. All I hear now is a flat, dead tone. I'm not sure what that tone means but given the broadcast I just watched, it doesn't sound like the emergency services will be much help to me now. I replace the phone in the cradle and check the time. Five minutes have passed already. I must have lost a few to the shock.

I leave the study, quietly closing the door behind me and poke my head around the lounge door. Tilly has assembled quite the little castle with her blocks and is re-enacting some sort of violent rescue as far as I can tell. Her homemade princess doll, which she named Ayla despite my protests, is the subject of the rescue. I manage a smile when she notices me and scans my face again with those heartbreaking eyes, and back out of the room.

What am I going to do about my parents? I love my mother dearly and want nothing more than to be able to help her or at least ease her suffering, but if the silver haired man is to be believed, the more contact I have with them, the more danger I put Tilly in, and I suppose, myself.

I approach their door and the sickly sweet stench has permeated the air outside in the hallway. I imagine it as a creeping fog in my mind's eye, and I swear I can almost see it. My heart skips and stutters in my chest. What if that is how it spreads? By the stench in the air? Am I already exposed? Almost certainly. I've had direct contact with them both and literally pulled a key from my father's flesh. But Tilly? Maybe not. I have to do what I can to protect her.

I decide the best thing to do for now is to seal my parent's door to the best of my ability. We are not short of general supplies in this house, or at least anything that could be conceivably useful to my father, and I know we have ample supplies of duct tape.

I return to the study and take a good look around. If I were a set of keys, where would I be? Hanging in plain view on the wall as it turns out. Father clearly trusted enough in our fear of him to stay out of here in the first place. He wasn't wrong.

I snatch the keys and check the time. Fourteen minutes to the next broadcast. As I exit the back door I pause, and fear grips me. The broadcast clearly told me not to go outside, but did not tell me why. If it's because of risk of contaminating others, that's a moot point. My nearest neighbours are miles away. If it's risk of exposure myself, well I'm as exposed as can be. I shake off the paralysis and force myself to step forward. The air has a funny quality to it, almost like a heat shimmer, but it's not nearly hot enough for that. My throat feels instantly dry and my eyes are watering a little. I ignore the unusual sensations and head toward the large garage set a little behind the house. It holds my father's stockpiles of everything and anything, as well as his truck and scrambler bike.

My hands are trembling as I pop the padlock off and my hand slips as I turn the handle. Feels almost gritty. I step inside and ignore everything except the pyramid of shining black rolls piled halfway to the ceiling. Usually the illicit thrill of being in here unsupervised would have had me running from stockpile to stockpile, examining the contents, but panic is rising in my chest at the thought of that bad air getting to Tilly, so roll in hand, I dash back the house. My feet seem to be sliding on the ground more than usual, but I pay this little heed.

I spend the next ten minutes tearing off lengths of tape and sealing every gap around the frame of my parent's bedroom door. I tape over the keyhole and then tape a second layer over the first, for good measure. I lean my head against the door for a few seconds. My poor mother. She never deserved any of this.

Tilly is still thoroughly absorbed in her imaginary world when I slip back into the study and close the door quietly behind me again. I check the clock. Two minutes to broadcast. I seat myself in the comfortable chair facing the television set, take a deep breath, and-

# Chapter Seven

*The other guy is in trouble. He knows it. His plan of poisoning that wretched beast failed miserably. The whore is convalescing in peace and comfort, while he suffers, sleeping in the dirt, eating spiders and insects rather than his preferred roasted lizard for fear of them seeing his fire. He was certain that the beast would come for him, but it merely sits at the entrance to the whore's cave. This much he can see through his binoculars from his vantage point. He shifts his weight and a lance of pain travels through him, originating in his arm but seeming to spread through his whole body. He is warm, far too warm, and yet his skin is bone dry. His mouth tastes chalky. What remains of his arm throbs relentlessly, each beat of his heart pulsing pain further and further up the limb.*

*He knows it must be infected. What he doesn't know, is what to do about it. He suspects that this arm will kill him sooner or later. A small part of him knows that there is another option, but does not want to think about that just yet. He knows the whore has a number of supplies, and perhaps among those supplies there will be a medicine that can help him. He just needs more time.*

\*

When I wake again the sun is setting, casting golden light over the camp. Hope is still stationed at the entrance to my cave and she gives me a perfunctory glance when I stir. I sit up and groan. The sharp pain in my ribs has graduated to a deep, dull throb. It might be an improvement, but it's still damned painful. I hobble to the mirror again. I feel like an old woman. My entire body is aching and stiff, and I feel uncomfortably hot, as though I am recovering from the flu. Normal flu that is. With or without Hope's help, my injuries will inevitably need more time to heal.

I give myself a quick examination. I was hoping to see the same level of miraculous improvement as this morning and am disappointed. The bruises are more green than blue now but that's about it. I'm still incredibly tender and while a heavy ache is an improvement on the sharp lances of pain of this morning, the ache seems to be a constant factor and is in itself almost more wearing. Hope has left me a fresh large lizard to roast and I get it cooking as quickly as I can, though I have little appetite. I know I must eat though, if I am to continue healing, so I force down the legs and a few pints of water. I try a few stretches but am forced to stop pretty quickly. I'm just *so tired.*

I lean against the cave wall, enjoying the first cool wind of the evening against my brow. Hope trots up to me and nudges my shoulder. *Track. Chase. Kill.* It's not quite as though the words are landing in my brain, more the impression of the word, the *feel* of the word. The dead lizard of this morning appears in my mind's eye, surrounded by an aura of *danger, threat, caution!*

I sigh and meet Hope's gaze. "Please Hope. I can't come with you yet. I can barely walk. I don't know how well I can protect myself. Please don't leave me."

Hope lets out an odd little huff, a sound almost human in its nature. *Impatience. Resignation.* She seats herself next to me and I lean into her hulking shoulders. I feel her nuzzle my hair. *Protection.* I smile. We sit there together for a little while, watching as the sunlight is chased away and the moon rises. It starts getting a little chilly. I suspect this wouldn't usually bother me anymore, but my aching, healing body feels everything today.

Despite my slight discomfort at the dropping temperature, I feel myself begin to drift off again, sleep coming in waves with the darkness. I stand and shake my head, trying to clear the thickening cobwebs. I don't feel ready to sleep again. These dreams, memories, whatever they are, are exhausting in themselves. But I'm stumbling and tripping over my own feet as I walk around, trying to keep myself awake, and my toe catches a rock, sending me tumbling face first into the dirt. I lay still for a moment, gasping to regain the wind that was knocked from me, trying not to inhale dust and dirt in the process.

I roll onto my back as soon as I am able and of course Hope is there, looking down into my face anxiously. She doesn't look it of course but I feel anxiety rolling off her in waves. I attempt to smile at her but all I manage is a grimace and a groan at the fresh pain this movement generates. Hope leans down and before I can turn my head or shut my eyes, catches me across the face and eyes with a sweep of her great tongue.

"Cheers Hope," I mutter, wiping globs of saliva from my eyes and cheeks. "That stings like a *bitch!*" It really does. My vision is blurring from a combination of tears and saliva and I wipe my eyes frantically as the sting grows more intense. Just when it reaches a level that seems unbearable, it begins to ease. I grope for Hope's shoulder and pull myself to my feet. I don't look at her. I'm sure she meant well, but I don't need any extra discomfort right now. My body feels like it's on fire as I wash down a couple more painkillers and roll myself up in my furs. I spare one last glance for Hope before my eyes shut of their own accord. She settles by the mouth of the cave as I raise the hand holding the remote and turn on the-

Television. The screen shows me an image of a monstrously large dog, silhouetted against moonlight for a second, before fading into the silver haired man. A smaller square at the bottom left of the screen holds the image of a young man with large glasses, who looks to have aged ten years in two days. Haggard would be the best descriptor for both men visible on my screen. Both men look incredibly grave. The silver haired man introduces the younger man as Dr Johnson, to no one's surprise.

Without preamble, Dr Johnson tells me that they have identified Bubble Flu as an incredibly aggressive new strain of virus. There is no hope for a cure or vaccine. Many people will die. It is spreading too fast to contain.

The silver haired man asks what can be done for those suffering from it. Dr Johnson replies that there is very little. The

most severely affected won't even take water. Some die of dehydration before respiratory failure.

"What causes the respiratory failure?"

Dr Johnson hesitates, seems to hold his breath for a second before letting it out in a big rush, almost tripping over the words. "Autopsies indicate that the bubbling rash spreads on the outside until it reaches the inside."

"Reaches the inside?"

"Yes."

"You mean the rash spreads to the lungs?"

"That is what I mean, yes."

The silver haired man stares at him for a few seconds. He mops his brow with a handkerchief pulled nimbly from his sleeve and lets it drop to the desk in front of him, clearly past caring about decorum. The sweat springs back as swiftly as he wiped it, beading over the powder applied to his face. A drop rolls south of his cheek, clinging to the edge of his jaw. My eyes follow its path with idle interest, waiting for the men to resume talking. The drop detaches, dropping to the lapel of his once immaculate dark suit. It leaves a small, milk coloured patch, contrasting with the smooth, navy darkness. I notice dozens of other small, lighter patches grouped around his shoulders, collars and lapels, and understand the man is sick.

Dr Johnson eyes him sadly. He can see it too.

"Do we know how it spreads?" asks the silver haired man, before doubling over into a harsh coughing fit, ducking under the table to hide.

Dr Johnson waits for him to surface before replying. "We initially assumed that the virus was spreading from person to person by the usual methods. Through the air, by touch, contact with contaminated effluence. But the virus when studied shows nothing to support this theory. It is not like anything we have seen before."

"What does that mean? Are you saying it's not contagious? It's spreading like wildfire!"

"Yes. But not from human to human, or human to animal, or animal to human. We believe it is carried by The Dust."

The cadence and the emphasis of his tone told me better than any subtitles that he used that as a proper noun. He's not talking about any old dust here.

"The dust?!" Incredulity saturates the reply of the silver haired man, even as he chokes on the words and ducks back out of sight, coughing violently into his stained handkerchief.

"Yes. The Dust. Our new advice is for people to stay indoors to avoid contamination. It is likely unnecessary to quarantine the sick and dying." Dr Johnson paused for a few seconds, gathering himself. "However it is apparent that exposure, perhaps on a global level, commenced approximately four days ago, when the first incidents of sickness were reported. Reports of an unusual type of dust started coming to us at the same time. The connection wasn't made until yesterday evening, when we started running tests on The Dust. It is somehow carrying live viral particles as part of its organic structure. We don't know how. The men who were working on identifying The Dust have all died in the last hour."

The silver haired man stares at him, mouth agape, any pretence of keeping up appearances for the camera departed. Sweat is running off him in rivulets now, his face is sheet white with angry roses blooming in his cheeks. His suit is beginning to look like a bad tie dye job.

Dr Johnson continues, even as the silver haired man is attempting to form a sentence. "The likelihood is, everyone is infected by now. There may be those who survive, if their body can fight the virus before the rash spreads to their lungs. Some may die of other factors such as dehydration, even without the rash spreading fully. There has not been enough time to estimate survival rates, as we have yet to see someone contract it and fully recover. Our researchers are all dying. I will be returning to my family once I have delivered this message, and I advise you to do the same." There is silence, for a few moments as the silver haired man processes this.

"You mean you're giving up? Who's going to fix it if not the fucking CDC?!" I doubt the silver haired man even remembers he's on camera at this point. He is standing, fists on the table, leaning in the direction of Dr Johnson, spittle flying at him as he vents his incredulous fury at the only man within reach he can blame. Dr Johnson stands and takes a step backwards, and that's when I see his hands, skin bubbling on both, and spy the rash hiding beneath the neckline of his white shirt. His face is still calm, sad and haggard, all at the same time.

"I rather suspect the world will fix itself, given enough time. The question of the human race will be answered too, when all is done."

With that bombshell, Dr Johnson exits stage left, and the screen cuts to black as the silver haired man collapses. The last image is of his skull bouncing off the side of his news desk, eyes rolled into the blackness of his own head.

I don't know how long I sit there, staring at the tv screen. My eyes see nothing, not that there is anything to see. The screen is a blank blue canvas. I feel the remote slip from my fingers, hear the thud as it bounces and settles on the threadbare carpet. I can hear Tilly, singing quietly in the lounge, saving her princess from the ogre she has fashioned to look suspiciously like our Father.

Dr Johnson's words roll through my head. "The likelihood is, everyone is infected by now...we believe it is carried by The Dust."

I recall the slippery feel of the ground outside, the odd, gritty slither of the handle as I gripped it. How harsh the air felt in my lungs and to my eyes. I try desperately to recall when Tilly was last outside. She likes to help Mother and I with the chores and my mind presents me with an image of Tilly, only yesterday, bundled up against the morning cold, tossing small handfuls of feed to the eager chickens pecking at her feet. She turns to me with that trusting, heartbreaking smile once her little apron was empty, the cold light of the rising sun gleaming in her golden hair and bright blue eyes and I scoop her tiny body into my arms and kiss the crown of her head. Like that we stay for a few minutes, drinking in the sight of that gorgeous sunrise, before I hurry her indoors, fearful of exposing her to the cold for too long.

Little did I know how misplaced my fear was. I tell myself to stand, to move, to take some action to protect her. But my body is numb, paralysed, helpless. Fear consumes me. Not for myself, but for my sweet, trusting, gentle little girl, who already knows too many of the horrors of life.

After what may have been a matter of seconds, minutes or even hours, I shake my head violently and push myself to my feet. I can check on my parents at least, now I know it won't harm Tilly any further. I close the study door in my wake and glance through the door to the lounge, satisfying myself that Tilly is still playing, undisturbed by thoughts of death or dying, before pulling that door closed as well. I set myself to tearing the duct tape seal from my parent's bedroom door, the sweet stench thickening as each strip of tape comes free. I open the door and am instantly engulfed. The thick air seems to solidify in my lungs and I struggle to draw breath, my eyes tearing up as I choke on the inhale. A gust of fresh wind pushes its way through the open window and I expel the air from my lungs, tasting rot under the sickly sweetness, and greedily inhale this fresher air.

I take a few steps into the room, aiming for my mother, eyes still adjusting to the dim room. And stop short. My parent's faces are both unrecognisable, covered in that creeping, boiling, bubbling rash. I see no movement from Father's chest at all, and as my eyes light on him, I see the skin of his face is beginning to slough sideways. I flip on the bright overhead light and step closer. His heavy jowls are pulling at the skin of his cheeks and as I watch they begin to separate, skin stretching like melted cheese, exposing the rotten teeth beneath. His jaw hangs open, stretching impossibly far with the slackness of death. My stomach clenches, acid rises in my throat and I'm compulsively swallowing the saliva flooding my mouth. I snag his stained shirt off the floor and toss it over his face. *Breathe Ayla.*

I sit beside my mother. Her chest moves, barely, and I hear her breath rasping and rattling. Her face has been consumed by the rash and I see that it has extended inside her mouth. Hers seems a little different to Father's. More solid somehow. I dare not touch it but his seems...gooey, for lack of a better word. As though the structure of the skin itself broke down in the process. Her rash is still awful, but her skin seems unbroken. Not that it matters. She is in her final moments and I take her hand, which is thankfully free of blisters, and whisper nonsensical words of comfort and love. Her fingers grip mine ever so slightly, and she is gone.

I sit with her then, grieving for this woman who though she could not protect me, loved me as best she could. Who taught me our history in whispered snatches through early morning toil, over bubbling cooking pots, words masked by squawking chickens and lowing cows as she painted pictures in my mind to help me make sense of the cruel world I was born into. Who passed on what knowledge she obtained before her right to education was withdrawn. Concepts of freedom and strength and equality that she secretly held onto even after being reduced to a mere possession. She held these for my sake. She did her best for me. For us.

When my tears cease flowing I stand, needing to compose myself. I cross to the window and shut it, drawing the curtains, and find my feet sliding ever so slightly across the wooden floor. My hands shimmer slightly in the light glaring from the bulb overhead and I realise I am coated in dust, as are the bodies of my parents and the floor. I realise then that I left the door open the whole time I sat grieving and cross to it hurriedly, wiping my face as I step into the hall and close the door behind me. Or at least, that's what I try to do. Rather than wiping cleanly off my skin, the dust seems to have coagulated when combined with the tears and sweat that had flooded my face, forming a sticky layer that clings to me painfully.

I duck into the bathroom and peel the mixture of dust, sweat and tears from my face, wincing as the fine, downy hair on my face comes with it. I resist the urge to scrub frantically as slowly, painfully, the makeshift mask lifts from my skin. My skin looks raw, the blood close to the surface of my fair skin. I am giving myself a final wash with soap and water when Tilly's shriek reaches my ears and pierces my heart. "Ayla! *AYLA!!*"

I bolt from the bathroom, note that my parent's door is still closed, though my feet slide on the dust that blew in while I sat by my dead parents. Bursting through the lounge door I drop to my knees beside her, frantically scanning the room for the source of danger, reaching for her to draw her close and protect her. She pulls away from my grasp, shaking her head, still shrieking my name in sheer panic.

"What is it Tilly? You have to be brave and use your words now, what is scaring you?" My words are sharpened by my own panic, rapping out like blows, the antithesis to my usual gentle, soothing tone when speaking to her.

My harsh tone stops her in her tracks, and her little face crumples. My heart cracks as fresh tears slide down her cheeks and her eyes drop, focussing on her little round tummy. She raises those swimming eyes back to mine and speaks the words that freeze me to the core.

"I have an icky Ayla and it *hurts*." Ickies are what Tilly calls any rashes or skin complaints. I always figured this was driven by revulsion of my Father's abundant eczema, which would leave trails of papery white skin in his wake. He would scratch for hours at a time, not caring if he drew blood, then stand and shake the disembodied skin off his clothes, powdering the room and anyone in it. It's a visceral sight, and one that stays with you. There's nothing like the feeling of breathing in your relations.

"Let Ayla see sweetheart," I moderate my tone as much as possible, and some of the tension lifts from Tilly's tight little shoulders. As she lifts her tunic to show me her belly, I note the sheen to her forehead, the glassiness to her eyes. The pallor of her skin, except for her cheeks, which flame with spots of colour. And drifting outwards from her bellybutton, the bubbling, deadly rash.

*

The first thing that registers when I fight my way out of my semi-drugged slumber is how cold and damp I am. Both myself and my furs are drenched with cold sweat. I must have been thrashing frantically in my sleep. My face is dripping and judging by the heavy sting in my eyes and congestion in my sinuses, I was crying as well. Hope comes to me when I ease into a seated position and lays her head in my lap. I throw my arms around her neck and shoulders and find my eyes pouring again, half choked shuddering sobs racking my body and waking my injuries anew as I cling to the one comfort I have, and I grieve again for the loss of the life I loved so much and knew so briefly.

Why am I now reliving this most painful time in my life? I've never forgotten Tilly or Mother, not really, but the passage of time blunts that knife, grief. The pain blends with the love until you can hold both in the same place and understand that truly they are one and the same. But slumbering in the depths of those memories, still so vivid, I feel that agony afresh as though it happened just yesterday. I have lived through this horror once, dammit!

I have no wish to see the life leave Tilly's body again but images enter my mind unbidden, of fever bright eyes and cheeks, her waxy pale forehead, glistening with that sweet, milky sweat. Her pain and confusion in those last few hours before she finally, blessedly drifts into slumber. Cradling her in my arms as her breath grows shorter and harsher, rasping in and out of her struggling lungs. My tears, falling thick and fast, mingling with the sweat that drenches her, anointing her with my love even as I know it will do nothing to save her. Finally, holding her in her moment of passing, singing her our lullaby, the one I made just for her.

*Sleep and rest where you are safe,*
*My darling dear close your eyes,*
*There's a place in my embrace,*
*Where nightmares flee and no one dies.*

*I'll circle you within my arms,*
*And surround you with only my love,*
*No pain, no fear, only still calm,*
*I'll shield you with my love, my love.*

That frail little body, tiny in life and somehow so much smaller in death.

After some unknown length of time, I begin to calm, taking deep, ragged breaths until my breath no longer hitches in my throat. Hope stays with me, her presence calming me as I wipe my face and blow my nose. Holy shitfire, but my eyes don't half *itch.* I'm rubbing at them, hoping to alleviate the sensation but it increases in intensity until it mirrors the sensation of Hope's saliva the night before and tears are once again streaming from beneath my lids. As the itching turns to pain and the pain reaches its fiery crescendo, I feel the most curious sensation, as though something has slipped into place over my eyes, and as suddenly as it came, the pain is gone.

I blink a few times, open my eyes. It is still dark inside and outside my cave but it may as well be blazing sunshine. I can see *everything.* Even from my vantage point at the rear of my cave, I see the veins and creases on the individual leaves on trees and bushes dozens of meters away. I zero in on movement very close to the ground just ahead of the treeline and marvel as I identify it as a small spider, scurrying about its business. The more I look, the more I see and my God! I may as well have been blind before today.

My eyes return indoors, settle on Hope and look her square in those golden eyes. Have I ever truly seen anything before? I'm struck dumb by the depth and beauty of those eyes, the rippling folds of shimmering ochre and topaz that curl through the clear, bright gold. I lose myself in waves of wonder and I could almost go mad from the beauty of it, when Hope's consciousness reasserts itself in a wave of smugness. No questioning that feeling. If I hadn't already made the connection, it leaves no question as to who's responsible for this latest evolution in myself.

I smile at my lovely girl, the spell broken, and I nearly feel like myself again, grief and aches and pains and all. Eager to examine my eyes, I leap from my bed, earning myself a jolt of pain from my ribs to remind me that I am nowhere near healed yet. Ignoring it the best I can, I flip on my lights and settle cross legged before my ancient spotted mirror.

My face is still a symphony in shades of peacock, but I barely register the mottled range of colours on my skin. The light dances off the surface of my eyes as though they're made of glass instead of flesh and flowing outwards from the inky black centre are waves of that pure, bright gold, bleeding into my original, cerulean blue. The effect is mesmerising, like a starburst exploding from the pupil, ringed with deep blue, and threads of gold, ochre and amber starring from the centre to just brush the edges of my irises. I wonder if the gold will continue to bleed through my whole iris, like Hope's, or if that last part of my own color will remain.

My irises are bigger than they were. The pupil seems permanently dilated, and yet I am able to see much more of the iris than I usually would. I glance over my shoulder at the lady of smug, lounging behind me with delicate grace.

"All the better to see you with my dear!" I call out, and dissolve into peals of laughter. When my mirth subsides (and it has been far too long since I've had something to laugh about), I examine my eyes again. I have an overwhelming urge to touch the surface of my eye and when I do, I find that the surface is indeed reminiscent of glass. I tap it with a fingernail and the sensation is akin to the feeling of tapping the surface of, well, a fingernail. I can feel it, but as though through a hardened layer. Incredible.

I stare directly into the lightbulb above the mirror and then immediately switch my gaze to the darkness outside the cave. There is no discomfort from looking at the light: on the contrary my eyes seem to drink in every detail, seeing everything from the glowing filaments at the centre to the dust motes hanging in the air, illuminated by the streams of light. When I look into the darkness, there are no blank spots in my vision blinding me and my eyes instantly adjust, allowing me to make out my surroundings with perfect clarity. What a gift she has given me!

"Thank you Hope. It seems I will never run out of things to be grateful to you for." She doesn't answer me of course. But I know she feels the gratitude  and love emanating from me and as I lean against her lustrous fur in contentment and peace, I feel an answering nudge that feels very much like, *you're welcome.*

# **Chapter Eight**

*The other guy shivers in the hole he has dug, in an attempt to protect himself from the encroaching cold. He has covered himself in a drift of dead leaves and dirt, hoping for insulation, but the cold leaches through and he trembles relentlessly. He is aware in some part of his mind that it's not all that cold, that his body is sick and the cold comes from within, but the heat emanating from his skin in spite of the tremors that seize him confuses him. Several days have passed with him watching the whore and her beast and he knows that the beast must come for him soon, just as he knows he will die soon without aid. He has only one advantage remaining to him; the weapon tucked into his belt, jutting into his spine. He dare not remove it to give himself more comfort. He fears in his addled state that he will forget its placement and lose the one weapon he still possesses.*

*He drifts in and out of disturbed sleep, his fever racked body and brain hurling violent, terrifying dreams into his mind. He flees from monstrous beasts, is trapped in fiery hellscapes, and thrashes and moans in his slumbering terror. The sound reaches the ears of that which he fears the most, standing guard next to the dreaming form of her precious mistress. The great creature seems to ponder, looking first at the woman sleeping, and then out into the surrounding darkness. After a few moments of what would seem like contemplation, she pads out softly into the night and is swallowed by the dark.*

*Some instinct, long dormant, which warns of creatures who prowl in the darkness outside the light of the campfire, giant, long toothed monsters who preyed on those early humans, rouses the other guy, who finds himself instantly, painfully, alert. It is coming for him. It is time.*

\*

Bands of pain clamp around my midriff, undulating, constricting, *squeezing*. Steel bars of agony tightening around my distended belly, arriving in waves, like the cruelest tide, returning every few minutes with increasing intensity. I roll onto my side, screaming for my mother, as a gushing flood of hot liquid departs from between my thighs, feeling as though it should scold me.

She rushes to my side, Father casting a shadow over both of us from the doorway, and kneels by my low bed. Her hands, small, cracked and rough from years of work and exposure to the harsh elements, brush my brow and take my hand. Her voice, quiet and low but rough edged with urgency, asks what ails me and as I open my mouth to answer, another wave of pain clamps around me and only screams leave my mouth, stretched wide in agony. I grip her hand so hard I feel the bones grind together under the skin.

She winces but does not pull away, and as I howl, waiting for this wave to recede, she lifts the blankets from me. She touches the spreading wetness beneath my hips and her hand moves to my belly, feeling the contractions rippling across it and I see the moment the worry and confusion on her face gives away to horrified understanding. She looks at Father with pure venom in her eyes, tells him to ready the truck, that I must go to hospital. He waits a moment before crossing the hall to his study, communicating to her without the need for words that she will pay dearly for that look, the delivery of those words, at a later time.

My mother turns back to me and strokes my brow, murmuring reassurance, assuring me that I will be ok, but I see the tears shimmering in her eyes and am sure that I will die, for what else would motivate my reclusive father to take me into the outside world? What possible affliction could cause me such pain and still allow me to draw breath when it has finished ravaging my body? It feels as though some ravening beast is tearing me from the inside out, chewing its way through my organs, flesh and bone.

I open my mouth to beg her to share her knowledge with me, but Father's shadow has returned, casting over us both and even in the midst of this pain so awful, fear closes my throat and snuffs out my words. He steps into the room, takes my arm in a vice-like grip and drags me from my bed. More fluid gushes from me when I am pulled upright and my bare feet slip and slide in what I am convinced must be my viscera, sending me halfway to the floor before Father's hand jerks me upright.

His knuckles crack across my cheekbone, snapping my head back, and I nearly fall again, but the pain barely registers next to the morass of agony that has gripped my centre once more and my knees buckle despite my best efforts. I dimly register him snarling at me, "Look at the fucking mess you've made you filthy bitch," before another blow mashes my lips against my teeth. He releases my arm and I drop to my knees, about to fall all the way down when he wraps his fist in my waist length hair and drags me out that way instead.

Mother follows us out to the truck, wringing her hands frantically, breath clouding in the autumn night air. We reach the truck, me clinging desperately to his wrist, trying to take some of the pressure from my scalp before he tears it from my skull and instead of opening the door to the cab, he unlatches the rear end of the flatbed and hurls me into the back of the open truck bed, slamming it back into place when my feet had barely cleared it.

"Bobby you can't leave her back there! It's twenty miles to the hospital she'll freeze! She doesn't even have shoes or a coat!" My mother calls across the yard, fear and panic choking her voice.

"I don't want that fucking shit on my seats. She'll survive. Probably." With that Father hops into the cab of the truck and roars out of the yard, me rolling around in the rear, clinging to the sides for purchase when possible but losing my grip every time another convulsion wracks my body, seeming to come with greater frequency all the time. The journey seems endless and when Father pulls me from the bed of the truck and drags me by my arm through giant glass doors that seem to open by magic, I become aware of a massive sensation of pressure, building around my pelvis.

I'm not cognisant of much after this. Men in blue clothes blur around me in a hive of activity as I'm lifted on to a bed and rolled into a gleaming white room. My feet are placed in stirrups and my sodden underthings are cut from me, leaving me exposed, vulnerable, helpless. Alien fingers probe my most private places, spreading me apart, *reaching inside of me.* Harsh voices cut through the pain dulling my senses, telling me I must push now, push, *push harder you silly girl,* but I don't understand what they mean, what they want, what is happening to me! Some sort of instinctive response takes over and I find myself bearing down as though using the bathroom. A vein of fire lights in my groin and tears through me, a new type of pain, even worse than before, and I'm screaming so hard that my voice cracks and tears and I feel something rupture in my throat at the same moment that something ruptures down below.

As I strain and scream and wrestle with whatever it is that is tearing me apart, Father's voice drifts to my ears, low, guttural and cruel. "Thirteen years old...probably been whoring around with some local farm boy...warned her what would happen if she didn't keep her legs closed but did she listen?"

I don't understand what he means. What farm boy? As my mind turns his words over, trying to wrest some sense from them, I am distracted by one final, massive burst of pain. I bear down with all my might, feel as my flesh is stretched and torn asunder, and as suddenly as it came, the pressure is gone and I am cold, shivering and empty, as though my insides have been scooped from me and pulled away. I hear a *snick,* somehow fleshy and metallic at the same time and can see the vague shape of the man between my legs, that harsh voice that had ordered me to push, come to his feet and turn from me, holding something in his arms.

My vision dims, darkness unfurling, and in my last moments of consciousness I am pierced by a sound, both alien and achingly, instinctually, *instantly* familiar. The cry of a newborn child.

*

I bolt upright, heart hammering, once again drenched in the icy cold sweat that follows the dreams of remembrance. Was that a gunshot I heard or did waking so suddenly play a trick on my senses? My hand instinctively drops to my empty stomach as memories once again crowd my mind, warring for dominance. Waking from that initial blackout to the sound of men offering to 'deal with it' for my father. Him musing about the cost and burden of raising another child, since 'that whore' would be incapable. The burning pain between my thighs warring with the cold emptiness that seemed to fill my abdomen.

Men with cold eyes gazing at me dispassionately, remarking on how thoughtless and irresponsible this generation of girls are turning out to be. Offering condolences to Father for the burden of such a thankless, worthless child. Father leaning down to the level of my ear and grimly promising that my child would be slung into an incinerator if words passed my lips of her true origin. For of course, this child was his as much as mine and up to the point of her being torn from my flesh, my ignorance of these matters precluded me from even knowing of her existence.

My mother would later explain to me that I had carried the child unusually, quite far back in my abdomen, and that combined with her premature birth and  my lack of usual symptoms, meant that my pregnancy was barely visible, my bump small enough that Mother and I had assumed I had simply put on a little weight. I always wore shapeless, baggy clothes far too large for me in that time and I was far beyond the age of my mother bathing me, else she might have noted that the curve of my stomach was not in fact that of a teenager going through puberty, that the swelling of my breasts indicated more than just the natural progression of my hormones. I had only had two menstrual cycles prior to this, and my mother had not thought it unusual when they stopped so soon after starting, as she told me that it was not uncommon for girls to be highly irregular in their early years.

This and more she would whisper to me in the days after I returned to that dark, isolated farm house, nursing my child, my sweet, beautiful Tilly for as long as I was allowed. I nursed her through long winter nights, listening to the rhythmic slaps and pounding of flesh in the room next door, as Father relentlessly beat Mother as punishment for not somehow discovering my pregnancy and taking steps to 'deal with it'. The structure of her face was forever altered after that period. Her left eye would permanently droop and twitch and there was a curl to the same side of her mouth through which drool would always escape. Yet another reason for Father to mock her. Her nose was flattened and broadened and he knocked out most of her teeth, lending her mouth and jaw a sunken look. Her hands would now always tremble with palsy.

But the rape was carried out behind my closed bedroom door, or the outhouses where the animals were kept, and I never told her, for shame and for fear of the harm that would come to her, so how could she know? She in turn had yet to tell me of the facts of life that would have alerted me to my own fate, believing as she did that I would not have to deal with the advances of men for many years yet. She had told me little of anything up to this point, only passing on domestic knowledge and that of animal care, believing it would be easier for me to settle to this miserable life if I knew no better. It was a perfect storm of ignorance, and truth be told, the only person to blame for it all was the only person to not feel the consequences.

Mother would rectify my ignorance as much as she could over the next three years. In those quiet hours when Father slumbered or when our voices were comfortably covered by the sounds of cooking or cleaning, Father installed in front of the computer. She told me everything she could think of, education that she remembered from her time in school. How the world was before. She explained to me the political events that led to us becoming less than even third class citizens, worthless and powerless in the eyes of the law. She told me of a world that was far from perfect, but where things were improving, and the climate of racism, terror and xenophobia that resulted in Emperor Windross's initial election as President.

She told me of Windross's escalating attacks on women's rights. All funding to clinics which provided birth control and abortion was immediately stopped. Sex discrimination laws were repealed. Maternity leave and benefits were withdrawn. Meanwhile Windross poured double the previous amount into the military budget and increased troop numbers by fifty percent, and in a move that surprised many, doubled the pay and benefits of all soldiers who had any involvement in combat. He also extended those benefits further by offering the like of education grants to military children, completely free medical care for any and all proven relations and housing and catering to immediate family that was lavish in comparison to what came before.

He then defunded all state funded medical care outside of the military and withdrew any and all state benefits, while reducing taxes sharply amongst the working population. He reportedly increased the military weapons budgets and departments on a massive scale, paying for this by selling a number of these weapons to countries like Russia and North Korea. By all accounts, he was fairly chummy with their respective leaders.

The upshot of this was a massively increased and staunchly loyal army, almost all of whom were based on home soil. Troops in the Middle East were returned home en masse almost as soon as Windross was elected; another massive point in his favour. They were well fed, well funded, well staffed, and well, they had an awful lot of very advanced, very powerful weapons. They started patrolling in the cities, ostensibly to support the police, but there was never a question of who held the authority. There were beatings, rapes, a few murders. The police either turned a blind eye or found themselves out of employment with no hope of getting more work, with no benefits or support to access, usually with families to support. After a few months, no one took that position and after a few more, they started to join in.

A few prominent Democratic politicians attempted to rally support against him, in the hope of turning the tide for the next election, fielding an even tempered and well liked socialist as their candidate. The day of the election, the people of America awoke to occupation, by their own army. All towns, cities and villages were lined with policemen and soldiers, all ballot centres closed for business. People were shepherded into the hubs of their respective places of residency, where large screens had been arranged for their viewing pleasure, guns brazenly pointing in their direction from all sides.

On these screens, near enough the entire population of America watched as the politicians remaining in the Democratic party, and a few naysayers in the Republican party, are all executed by firing squad.

Windross then inducted himself as the first Emperor of the United States and declared his intent, that any American man will now live as he pleases, so long as he provides for himself, and doesn't bring harm to a fellow American man. This protection applies to no one else on American soil. Women and any of those remaining of the immigrant population, few as they were now, came under the regulation of American men, who could do with these parties as they pleased. Those who objected were shot on the spot. The population fell in line. Women and the very few remaining non Americans became little more than slaves overnight, bound to the whims of whoever might claim them.

As Mother explained it, while there were of course decent men left who cared for the women in their lives the best they could, it was implicitly frowned upon to openly treat women well. Women were not allowed to work or pursue education. Unmarried women were open to being claimed, though if they had a living male relative that relative would have to agree to the claim. Wives of immigrant men were claimed, the men shot if they objected.

My mother was sixteen at the time of what she called the 'Big Change' when we spoke of it, capitals clearly implied in her tone. She was glad that she at least had that much time in education. Her father was always a wastrel as she told it, unemployed and panicking at the time of the change, watching his little money disappear on the cigarettes and booze that he would not give up even as his two daughters and wife grew smaller and thinner before his eyes. He jumped at the offer Father made of him of a couple of thousand dollars, selling his daughter without blinking an eye to a man already in his late thirties, while she was barely sixteen. Not even old enough to vote, had she still the right.

Father claimed her and immediately cloistered her in his inherited farm, beating and raping her daily until she conceived me. He was so furious at the birth of a daughter that when she came home from giving birth to me, he beat her viciously and tortured her, stamping repeatedly on her tender abdomen and genitals, forever damaging her. She never conceived again.

All of this she passed to me and more, always cautious of the wrong words reaching Father's ears, arming me with the only weapon she could give me. Her knowledge, her thoughts, and I suppose, her love. She always made sure I knew that she loved me.

Tilly was raised by Mother and Father in name, though of course the burden of her care fell almost entirely to me. But I was not to claim her as my own in her eyes, Father knowing of course how it would needle and pain me to hear her calling someone else Mother. He failed, after a fashion though, as it was always to me that Tilly would run when scared, turn to for comfort, share with her joy and show her greatest love to. She knew at the very least, that I loved her as much as a mother would love a daughter and as I brought her into the world, I held her when she passed from it.

The memories run their course and I am left again, shaken, cold and bereft. Why has this particular memory returned to me? I've been off the painkillers for the last three days, as my healing injuries pain me less, and I have slowly returned to my usual habits. Taking it easy on the harder exercise of course and not venturing far from my camp, but I've cleaned and repaired all my equipment, replenished my stocks of dried meat and berries, purified and stored lots of extra water and cleaned and serviced the engines on both my bike and the truck I keep close by. My bruises have mostly faded to hues of sickly yellow and green and the pain has lessened to a dull throb that I barely notice for the most part. So why the sudden flood of recollections?

My hand still rests on my stomach, and I can feel a thought, just out of reach, almost tickling my mind. The answer to my question, there, taunting me. Pregnancy. Traumatic birth. A baby.

Am I pregnant? Is this what my subconscious is trying to hammer me over the head with? They told me after Tilly was born that the damage caused to my body by her traumatic labour would prevent me from conceiving again. My mother suspected something more nefarious, that they had done something to me in the aftermath while I was unconscious at Father's request. Either way, as far as I know, I cannot conceive. I certainly did not conceive again, though Father would rape me several times more between Tilly's birth and his death.

The question continues to niggle at me however. What if? What if the changes my body has gone through over the last ten years, and particularly these last few months, has served to heal previous damage done? I have found myself examining my new, harder skin for scars that I know once existed, but other than my current collection of bruises, my skin is now unmarked and smooth. If the surface can heal old scars, why not beneath the surface? Is this paranoia or is my subconscious giving me a genuine message here?

A chill rolls over me and settles heavily as I consider this possibility, and the consequences. Another chill serves to freeze me to the core when I look around my humble dwelling and realise that Hope is gone.

# Chapter Nine

How long have I sat here, unaware, lost in my memories? I last saw Hope as I drifted to sleep last night, standing guard over me as she always does when I sleep. I feel as though it was still full dark when I bolted from my disturbing nightmare and now I see the first fingers of dawn caressing the ground outside.

I call out to her, standing in the mouth of my cave, eyes scanning my surroundings for any sign of her. I easily pick out her tracks leading out of the clearing and a few feet into the wooded area that surrounds my home, but then I lose her almost immediately. A few snapped twigs and disturbed leaves tell me that she took to the trees, but after scrambling up myself, there is nothing more in the way of spoor for me to follow. I lower myself back to the ground and stare at the offending tree in consternation. Damn her and her tree scaling skills, and damn her for leaving me like this!

I can feel the anxiety knotting my stomach and tightening my chest as I walk back, trying and failing to control my breathing and heart rate. I try to reassure myself. Whenever I have panicked before, she's come running straight back to me. Surely this time will be no different. I try to *push* out with this feeling, call her back to me with this mysterious connection that we undoubtedly share, but I feel nothing, no answering nudge or tickle. I hear nothing. I see nothing. I try to keep my hands busy, cleaning my equipment, doing my stretches and exercises, eating breakfast, though stress and anxiety have robbed me of my appetite.

As the sun creeps higher I become increasingly aware of a curious emptiness beneath the tightness in my chest, as though something that was once there was missing. Something so intrinsic that its presence was notable only by its later absence. That curling, spreading warmth that made itself known many moons ago, the first night that I slept with Hope by my side, has gone, and with this realisation adrenaline floods my veins and fear begins to take hold.

I hurriedly pull on my gear, fumbling at the various straps and laces with fingers clumsy with panic. I grab my bowie knife and bow and arrows and bolt into the trees, starting at the tree where I lost Hope's trail, zipping through the woods in a state of ever increasing panic, desperately trying to see any sign, any mark, any*thing* that might give me a clue as to the whereabouts of my dearest.

Fear clouds my mind and my senses until I may as well have been stumbling blind, tripping over roots and branches that I would have evaded without even a thought were my mind clear. The cold emptiness in my chest seems to grow larger and larger, until I am certain it must consume me. It seems to trap my air more and more with every breath I take, and now the air is whistling in and out of my lungs, my lungs are burning, my vision is clouded and gray and narrowing more with every second that passes.

Now I find myself on my hands and knees, staring at the ground and my hands, digging into the earth, fingers curled into claws, lungs now *screaming* for air. My vision narrows further until there is only darkness in my periphery, yet I see my hands in the earth with cold, crystal clarity. My hooked fingers have disappeared into the rich soil, breaking the velvety texture of the surface and crumbs of dirt and earth, deep brown and black, are scattered across the back of hands so tense that the tendons and veins stand out in relief. I can see my pulse throbbing, the earth shifting ever so slightly as my intrusion forces a worm out of its snug hiding place towards the broken surface.

I disturb a small wolf spider who skitters across my hands and realise that no, it's not a worm shifting the earth, it's a *centipede,* undulating its way beneath my palm and through the gap between my hands. My vision narrows to pinpricks now, still with that disturbing, razor sharp clarity, my lungs are *on fire* and the centipede seems to grow, bigger than my hands, bigger than *me,* and as it seems that I must surely die if I do not breathe, I vomit, copiously. Heaves rack my frame as my meagre breakfast is purged from me and I am finally able to draw a shuddering, ragged, painful breath, collapsing onto my side, just avoiding the pile of my leavings. I lay still, exhausted now, watching apathetically, idly, as the centipede, now garnished with the contents of my stomach, weaves its way back into the earth and *just for a moment*, I close my eyes.

\*

*The other guy has returned once again to his vantage point by the time she exits the cave and calls out for the beast to come to her. A savage, cruel, yet joyous sneer twists his face into something almost demonic, the pleasure evident in those curling lips and burning eyes growing with her anxiety, correlating with her panic. This is a pleasure that is sexual and yet still chaste. He stiffens and swells as he watches her but barely notices it, as the enjoyment he feels at the sight of her pain, her* emotional *pain, is so intense as to make other pleasures seem insignificant. The pursuit of this, her torment, her tears, her fears and now her swelling realisation that she may once more be alone in the world, gives such sweet gratification, is such a hedonistic high, that given the choice he would happily forsake sexual pleasure for eternity, in exchange for witnessing even fleeting moments of her despair.*

*A true sadist is he, the other guy, who understands that physical scars heal quicker than emotional ones. That the pain of broken ribs and a battered face will never outweigh the pain of a loved one lost. That time will erase even the nauseatingly shameful recollection of being invaded by an unwelcome appendage, but never that first, shellshocked, brutally clear moment of understanding that you will never see, touch or speak to your loved one again.*

*He follows her as she stumbles through the woods, at first keeping far enough back that he tracks her by sound, not sight, then closing the gap as it becomes apparent that she can barely see the ground before her through the fog of her panic. His unnoticed erection grows as her breathing becomes more laboured and he* rubs it with his good hand every few moments, seemingly unconsciously. He hangs back a little, watching through the gaps in the trees as she falls to her hands and knees, and wonders if her panic will kill her before he has a chance to do it himself. The thought makes his cock leap and he looks down, seeming surprised to find that he is now holding it loosely and he debates with himself, whether to just wrap his belt around her throat and fuck her again now, or to wait and hope she survives so he can savour the added pleasure of a long, drawn out hunt and the long, drawn out torture to follow. He notes with wry amusement that she has collapsed in the exact clearing in which he had hidden himself for days, and in which he had brought an end to her beast, only hours before.

She vomits then and manages to breathe, so he decides to wait. He closes the gap when she closes her eyes and looks down on her unconscious form, stroking himself, fully aware now of his lust and the realisation that he doesn't lust for her body, but for her suffering. He considers leaving his seed splattered across her face but thinks better of it. He is a more effective enemy if he is unknown after all, he muses to himself, and spurts into the puddle of vomit she left instead.

He does not know how long she will slumber for and with his lust sated, for the moment, he is aware once more that in a direct contest in his present condition, he would likely find himself defeated. His weapon he had discarded once discharged. He had no more ammunition for it after all. All he has now is his one good hand and both good feet, but attached as they are to his fever ridden, weak body, these feel like feeble weapons indeed. He could try to detach her bow and arrows from where they lie beneath her, and shoot her before she is able to disarm him. Or slide that wicked looking knife from its sheath on her belt and cut her throat. Or splatter her brains across the trees with any one of the handy fist sized rocks scattered around the bases of the trees. Kick through her temples with his heavy boots. Even kneel on her shoulders and choke the life from her with his working hand.

But that's not good enough for this guy, the other guy, the sadist who becomes more erect at the sight of her suffering than he *did at the sight of her bare rear and thighs and what lay between only days before. He wants to take his time and relish every drop of blood, sweat and tears that he draws forth before the end. He wants to break her, piece by piece, mentally, physically and emotionally until she begs him to release her to death. When he is ready, and sure that nothing of her strength, will or* fucking pride *remains, he will give her that release while buried in her depths, and feel her spasm around him in her moment of passing.*

*His cock twitches again at the thought, and he smiles, almost ruefully. He hasn't been as virile as this since he was a teenager! She is a whore indeed, to provoke such a response in him, he muses, and he walks back to her camp as quickly as his ravaged body will allow.*

*A quick search yields what he is looking for in one of the smaller caves near her main dwelling and he stuffs his empty pack with strong antibiotics and painkillers, clean bandages, tubes of antiseptic ointment, tins of meat, beans and fruit and a small bottle of whisky. He spots a large cache of water purifying tablets and snags a bottle of those too, along with matches, lighter fluid and a thick fur blanket. He spies vials of a clear liquid, syringes and needles, and a cursory examination identifies these as morphine. He is tempted, so tempted, to take some with him, to have some time completely free of pain, but he rightfully fears the consequences should he be discovered unconscious and in the grip of a drug so strong. Fuck it. He'll find a safe enough spot. It's not like the whore will be leaving this sweet setup anytime soon. He swipes a few of each.*

*He tries to rearrange things so that they don't appear disturbed, but his own head is growing foggy now, and he struggles to recall the original layout to emulate it. The adrenaline of the morning's events and endorphins from his episode of lust have long gone and the misery of his fever and pain of his injuries have reasserted themselves as his dominant sensations. He feels desperate for sleep and warmth but knows he must now go some way before settling again. She will likely scour the surrounding land for the next few days, searching for her beast, and he needs to grow strong again. He decides to head into the canyon proper and set up temporary camp in one of the inset caves, where he will feel safe to light a fire and convalesce if not in comfort, then at least in peace. He spots a fine example of a machete on his way out and hefts it experimentally. That'll do, for now.*

\*

Consciousness returns to me in drips and droplets, sensations trickling through fog, like grains of sand through an hourglass made of cloudy, impure glass. I am reminded of Father's hourglass, an old, twisted thing, made of dull, dark metal and yellowed glass. You could see the movement of the black sand as it patiently poured, ever moving down, but you could not see the grains themselves unless you and the light were perfectly positioned to allow it.

At first, I am only cold and heavy, weighed down by a feeling that both consumes and eludes me. A dull ache pervades my foggy head and flows through what eventually makes itself known as my neck and chest. I have no wish yet to open my eyes, but as that thought comes to me, I am aware that those eyes too feel heavy and swollen. I feel little else yet of my body and gradually I realise that my left side is almost completely numb. I try to shift, roll onto my back and my senses are immediately assaulted by the sharp pain that seems to dig into my spine and kidneys. I am lying on my bow and quiver. I free my favourite weapons with my working hand and roll over, successfully this time. The exposed skin of my face and hands burn with cold.

As a sensation not unlike fire ants crawling beneath my skin floods my numbed left side, I realise my clothes and skin are soaking wet and icy cold. Tremors so powerful as to be almost violent begin to rack my body, each contraction of my stiff, sore muscles triggering a fresh wave of burning pinpricks as the circulation returns to the numbed half of me. A gust of wind rolls over me and I am instantly more cold and wet, partly from the realisation that it is raining, heavily. Water pours through the trees above me so continuously that I had failed initially to separate the cold from its cause. It rarely rains in the summer months here, but when the autumn rains come they are so heavy that just being outside can make you feel like you're drowning with each breath.

I feel now the water pooling in the hollow of my throat, eyes and between my breasts. The rivulets pouring down my cheeks into my hair and the ground below. The soft earth beneath me turning to glutinous mud.

I open my eyes to a world of grey. My eyes and throat seem lined with that same sand that once flowed in the gloomy home of my childhood. Even through the rain water now pouring into my eyes, I can see the sodden branches and leaves that stretch overhead, and beyond them, the dark grey sky that seems to hang so low, its belly swollen with rain clouds and the ominous promise of thunder. Even as the thought drifts across my mind, the sky is ripped apart with a flash that should be blinding, followed immediately by sharp whipcrack and low pitched, guttural rumble that seems to shake the very ground beneath me. I smell the sharp, metallic tang of ozone and feel the curious sensation of every fine hair on my body rising to meet the crackling electricity that seems held in the air itself. A fresh squall of rain follows, now pouring so thickly as to impede even my preternatural vision.

I sit up, gingerly, but my body gives no further protest. The fire ants have withdrawn, replaced with only a light humming sensation, which fades itself as quickly as it came. I take in my surroundings now for the first time. I'm sat roughly in the middle of a small clearing, ringed by tall trees rendered monstrous by the low light and savage weather. The branches stretch overhead and provide what is almost a canopy, reinforcing that this rain must be heavy indeed, to be pouring so thickly through the natural barrier provided. I turn my attention to the ground. There is my vomit, almost washed away now. Large stones are littered around the roots of the trees and the ground is thickly carpeted with fallen leaves that in the sunlight would be a riot of colour, but are robbed of any such colour by the grey misery that is the light filtering through the clouds and branches above me. It is difficult to judge the time of day with such a barrier between the sun and myself, but the numbness I awoke to suggests a slumber of at least a few hours.

My eyes linger on the remains of my breakfast, swiftly dissolving and disappearing as I watch and as another pure white flash rips the sky apart, throwing everything into sharp, contrasted relief, the realisation hits me like a sledgehammer. This same rain will be washing away any sign that might inform me of the fate of my dearest. I squeeze my eyes shut and though they would be invisible amidst the rainwater on my skin, I feel the hot tears running in rivulets down my cheeks.

The sharp tang of ozone has faded from the air and my sensitive nose has become aware of another scent. I open my eyes and look around me again, with more purpose. The scent has mingled with the scent of wet earth, fresh and rotten leaves and of course my own vomit. Blood. A lot of blood. And beneath that again, I scent layers, of infected flesh, old leather and unwashed human. That almost cheesy reek. And just a faint, faint trace of...gunpowder. The other guy.

My sharp eyes, now seeking with fervour, spot a slight hollow surrounded by disturbed earth, and now I know that there is something to find, I see the trace outlines of footprint and faint scores in the earth that could have been made by long claws. Lightning floods the sky again and I'm looking in the right direction this time. The tree closest to the disturbance is starkly highlighted for me in the flash of light and I see the blood, dried to a dull black in that harsh light, splattered against the tree, and the somehow dull gleam of a bullet, embedded in the bark. The tree's trunk was more protected from the rain than the ground, and the blood must have had time to thoroughly dry before the storm arrived. I am on my feet and at the tree before I've even thought about it, and I kneel, sifting through the sodden leaves and earth with hands numb from more than just the cold, until I find what I fear.

A clump of brown fur, shot through with gold and auburn, and now matted with blood.

Feeling almost as though I am walking in a dream, I follow the path over which he dragged her body. The rain makes it fainter with every step that I take, but after a few hundred meters it becomes clear to me where it leads. For over the relentless beating of what seems like endless rain, another sound makes itself known, faintly at first, but louder and louder with each further pace, until it is a roar that nearly drowns out all other sound. Drowns. How appropriate. For I now stand at the bank of a roaring, rapidly flowing river, swollen to several times its prior volume by the sudden deluge from the heavens.

I need little confirmation that my beloved passed this way, but I look for it, to be sure, as the last hundred meters or so were across open ground, unprotected from the elements, and any spoor has been thoroughly washed away. I find it twisted in the thorny, scrubby bushes populating the river bank. More fur, torn from her as he dragged her through those bushes. One long, serrated claw that must have caught on the roots of the bushes. A scrap of bloody, stinking cloth hooked tight onto the thorns. My Hope passed this way, and now she is surely lost to me. My screams drown out even the thundering water and I howl until my throat feels as though it must bleed. With grief, loss, and sadness, yes, but also with an unbridled fury that goes beyond anything I have ever felt before.

I drop to my knees, scraping myself on small rocks and thorns and care for none of it, because is this not my fault also? If I'd have relented, tracked him down with her, then she would surely be alive and by my side right now. I found love and warmth after a decade of sheer loneliness, and I may as well have shot her myself. I am seized by a temptation then, so strong that I am crawling forward almost unconsciously, to follow her into that river and be done, with life and with pain. For there has been *so much pain* and I no longer wish to bear it, not alone, not having known the pleasure of loving company again after so long without.

The water rushes past me, so powerful, *so fast,* and I know I would not survive it long. I dip a hand into the water and the force almost knocks me over. My gaze drops and beneath my hands, stepped into the mud by a now just barely visible boot print, is a metal buckle, perhaps from a boot. I pluck it from the sodden earth, and turn it over in my hand. It is rusted a little, the tongue is missing and not even a scrap of fabric remains, but I am sure this belonged to the other guy, and on sight of it, my rage returns. My teeth clench, my heart rate spikes, the taste of copper floods my mouth and my fist closes tightly on this insignificant scrap of metal, squeezing so tightly that a drop of blood leaks from the edge of my furrowed palm.

I can kill myself later, if I still choose to, but even if it is with my very last breath, the other guy must die.

# Chapter Ten

It takes me a few days to realise that someone has disturbed my stores. The days after my grievous discovery are a mere blur of grief and fury, pivoting back and forth between hysteria in the form of howling tears, and a towering rage that seems to consume my very being. Grieving not only for my wonderful companion, who seemed imbued with so many human qualities that I had stopped viewing her as other to human long ago, but also for the loss of companionship and love, a loss felt all the more keenly for its absence before. Sure, I'd been alone before, but I'd never allowed myself to dwell on being lonely, as there was no other way for me to live, no alternative to grasp.

In my own way though, I am used to grief. I witnessed the death of my mother and my daughter, witnessed the dissolution of all civilisation. This grief, like those others, will pass, given enough time.

This rage though...this is something else. I've felt anger before, of course. Who hasn't? But the anger that came before was either provoked by fear, or a cold and calculated lens through which to plan the execution of vile men. It was never so consuming, so powerful, *so dark*. I've never been sadistic. I've always killed as cleanly as possible. But in these moments, minutes, hours of white hot fury, I feel capable of burning him alive, inch by inch, limb by limb, hair by stinking, greasy hair, and of burning the whole world with him if I choose. I want to bathe in his pain, anoint myself with his tears, and laugh as I scoop his eyeballs from his sockets, so my laughing, gloating face is the last image he will see.

The rage and grief soon coalesce, hardening under relentless pressure until it feels like a bright, white diamond in my chest, filling the space left empty when she was torn from me. Both painfully hot and icy cold, it sits, under my breastbone as a constant reminder of what has been lost and what must be done. And with the return of my sense of self, now harder, harsher and more cruel than the self that came before, comes the sharp, shocking reminder of what I must now do for myself.

For on the morning of the third day, I awoke not to the haze of tears and grey to which I was becoming accustomed, but to a sharp wrench in my gut, followed by a full hour of vomiting that was prodigious in nature. Having expelled what feels like every fluid in my body, and gingerly sipping some water, my hand drops to my sore abdomen, massaging my tender muscles, and stops short. There is a fullness to my lower abdomen that wasn't there before, more apparent perhaps than it would have usually been, as I have rather neglected my dietary needs whilst in the grip of my overwhelming grief. Between the dual jut of my pelvic bones, more pronounced now than they have been in years, lies a rounded protrusion, home to a parasite that has made its berth in me.

My instincts, dreams and now my body, tell me that I am forging a child, a child fathered by that Shit for Brains of all people, and this I cannot allow. For the longest time I had put the thought of carrying and birthing another child far from my mind. Like the prospect of love and company before finding my dear Hope, it was an impossibility, and as such, deserved no thought or dwelling. Do I want to bring a child into this terrible, terrifying world? I'm unsure. Do I want to bring *his* child into this bleak, unforgiving landscape? It is unthinkable.

Nearly two weeks have passed since receiving his vile offering. My body shouldn't even know if it is pregnant yet, let alone be showing any signs to confirm it, but I have my suspicions that like most things in our new world, this pregnancy will follow rules different to those which I am accustomed. Did I not witness Hope grow from a baby to her full, monstrous size in the space of only two months? We had dogs on our farm growing up, and my beloved childhood dog, Lilly, a large beast with a similar look and shape to Hope, took at least eighteen months to reach her full size, and enjoyed a further four years of life before she died.

Of course she died under my father's boot, her skull crushed for daring to bark at him when he raped me for the first time in the barn where we kept the cows and pigs. He returned to his pleasure when the deed was done and turned me to face the ruin of her beauty, so that I would understand the consequences of defiance.

It is fair then to assume, that I cannot trust in my prior knowledge and experiences of gestation and birth, or the growth that occurs afterwards. Perhaps this deadly virus which targeted warm blooded life, has changed the survivors on a genetic level, beyond just the improvements I have seen in myself. The future of humanity, if there is to be one, might look very different indeed.

Deep breath Ayla. Time to think. Time to plan. Time to act. The time for wallowing is past. I recall that there are medicines that will rid me of my concern, though of course I'd had no reason prior to this to know their names. I certainly have no intention of attempting those barbaric back-street methods of ending pregnancies that many of the women of my mother's generation were forced to fallback on. One of the many stories my mother told me was of the sharp decline in women's health care, access to contraception and abortions being one of the first rights to be withdrawn. They were still available, of course, but only with the permission of the woman's owner, be that her husband, father or in rarer cases, brother. They were a prop to the convenience of men, not an aid to the health and safety of women.

Many women had to resort to barbarism to rid themselves of unwanted pregnancies, many of which were of course conceived through rape. Not that rape was recognised as a crime anymore, or even a concept. Objects and possessions did not have rights or the ability to give or withhold consent. Mother heard tell of countless women who bled to death or died of infection following cold interactions with the grim faced men and women who offered these services, usually for significant sums of money, and mostly with unsanitised knitting needles that had perforated the wombs of many who had come before.

Those that survived, if caught, were generally beaten to death by their owners or publicly executed for 'desecration of the property of American men.' The owners, if they chose to turn the women in rather than killing them themselves, were given the freedom to choose the manner of execution. A popular choice was the ironically named, 'Death by Love'. The woman would be tied securely with her legs tied apart in a public area, and raped continuously by soldiers, police or even members of the public, until she bled to death, a process which could take several days.

No, we won't be doing any of that. I mean, I don't even possess a knitting needle, and I rather suspect a sewing needle, of which I have plenty, will not do the job. Luckily I scavenged an old dog eared copy of the Physician's Desk Reference many years prior, which has greatly informed my acquisition of drugs and medical supplies. I'm not just holding on to antibiotics and painkillers in my stash, though that makes up a significant proportion of it. I have local anaesthetics, benzodiazepines, blood thinners, anti-emetics, laxatives, antihistamines and epinephrine, activated charcoal, anticonvulsants and many more, as well as bandages and other supplies in every size, shape and form. Some of it seems pointless, in that I wouldn't have the required knowledge to know when to use it. But who's to say who I'll meet in the future years? Or what knowledge I may obtain for myself? I've near enough memorised my copy of Grey's Anatomy, a possession treasured nearly as highly as my PDR. If I find other books and materials in future, I can expand my knowledge further.

I do wonder how effective these traditional medicines will be on my changed body, especially since they are mostly, at least according to their label, expired. It doesn't hurt however to keep them on hand.

So while I don't have the required medicine here with me, I have the means to put a name to it. Then of course, I'll have to hunt it down, which could be a journey anywhere from a few days to a few weeks, depending on how far I have to go to find a hospital or medical centre that hasn't been completely ransacked and even stocks the medicine in the first place. The nearest hospital to me is located roughly thirty miles outside of the park limits, and is responsible for the majority of my stockpile, so that's the logical place to start.

I'll need to take supplies to last me a little while, but I'll also need to be sensible. Water in years gone by would have been my biggest concern, but my need for water has steadily reduced over the last few years and since meeting Hope, has reduced further still. While I needed roughly 1.5 - 2 litres a day ten years ago, I seem able to cope with half a litre or less now, even in the blistering summer heat. I function better with more, but can survive on less. The rain has lessened since the deluge of three days ago, but there are still regular, heavy showers and these will likely continue through most of the winter months. I will take a full litre bottle with me, and collect rainwater and river water where I come across it. A bottle or two of iodine to purify the water along the way, and that problem is solved.

It is tempting to take a truck and simply load it up with supplies, but a truck is far more likely to attract attention than my trusty electric motorbike, which runs almost silently, and without the need for fuel. It runs on a fine solar battery, which charges throughout the day from sunlight and also from the movement of the wheels. I can carry a spare too, just in case, which will take up little room in my saddlebags. Food will likely be more scarce in the open land than in the park itself, but I doubt I will have too much difficulty shooting or snaring myself a lizard a day. I can take dried meat and berries with me as a back up and I recall the box of high calorie dried protein bars I found on a supply run a few years back. They might not taste great but worse case scenario, one of those will get me through most of the day, and they take up little space all told.

There will be plenty of abandoned buildings to take shelter in at night if I choose, so I won't bother with supplies to sleep outdoors, but I'll take my sleeping bag, which rolls so tightly as to barely use any space at all, but which reflects the heat very effectively. That baby's kept me alive in rare minus temperatures in the past, and we won't be seeing cold like that for another month at least. No spare clothes, I'll have to forgo the pleasures of clean clothes and skin for a little while. I'll need to wear most of my defensive kit at all times too, but these pieces are so well made for me that this won't be a hindrance, and with the lowering temperatures and rain, I'll be glad for the extra layers, even if I am bothered by the cold so much less these days.

Practically speaking, I will be in constant danger, so remaining in my lightly armoured kit will be nothing but sensible. Which leads me to my most important supply. Weapons. I will of course take my bow and arrows, and these can be secured to the back of my pack when not worn, but they can't be accessed in a hurry when worn on my pack. I debate with myself whether to take the big pack at all. I can probably fit the required supplies into my saddlebags and carrier comfortably, and this way I can strap most of my weapons on to my person, making them accessible at any time. Filling all three will make the bike slower and more unwieldy, but it seems like the better option. I've modified the bike frame to carry a spare quiver of arrows too, and I can keep a hundred or so darts in a small section of lidded pipe I cut off and modified for the purpose.

I can use my smaller waist pack to carry provisions for times I'll need to leave the bike, without it hindering my bow, quiver and my favourite machete, which also has a home at my back, on the harness I made specifically for the three, as well as a sheathe on my jerkin, for the times that I don't take my bow and arrows with me. The chest straps provide a home for my blow gun and ten darts at a time, and the harness, which cinches at the waist, has a small sheathe on each side, holding two of my small, sharp bone knives. My belt then has a loop for my trusty hand axe and an additional two sheaths, one for the bowie knife and one for a dagger, of which I have several. And of course the bone knives sheathed in my boots. That plus my mods and at least I can be constantly well equipped as far as self defense is concerned.

Rough plan made, I dart into the first of my supply caves, to get the iodine and put together a small first aid kit, and am pulled up short. It is immediately apparent to me that someone has been here. My medicines, all neatly organised by type have been mixed and jumbled, and some stores have been depleted, though not significantly enough to worry me. A fur blanket is missing. My machete! My favourite machete, so well balanced and true, I had left near the entrance, I'm sure of it. I have spares, but that was by far my favourite. The lingering odour of infection, rot, grease and sweat would have given him away even had he left my supplies perfectly ordered. That man is nothing if not *pungent.* The other guy must have raided me while I was searching for Hope. Judging by the supplies he has taken though, and the odour remaining even now, the other guy is sick and in a lot of pain. There's definitely some morphine missing, as well as a lot of antibiotics, disinfectants and other painkillers. Guess that arm isn't healing so well. Shame. Maybe gangrene will finish him off before I get to him.

Or maybe not. He did after all survive over a week with that heinous injury, and have enough energy remaining to shoot her and drag her body over half a mile to that river, using only one hand at that. Now I don't know exactly how much my girl weighed, but she was roughly five to six times the mass of an average large, pre-apocalypse dog, if not more. I feel that I would find that difficult even now, with no injuries hampering me, and my estimation of the other guy as an opponent rises. Perhaps delaying my outward journey by a day or so and tracking him down now, while he is still weaker from his injuries, and I am almost at full power, would be the most sensible move.

I deliberate, unconsciously shifting my weight from foot to foot, tensing and relaxing different muscle groups, rolling my joints and stretching out as I weigh up the pros and cons. The accelerated rate of my pregnancy symptoms are a huge concern, and it could be days or weeks before I find my solution. This however seems too good an opportunity to miss. I should be able to track him with this as a starting point, between my sense of smell and keen eyes. It seems almost a shame that he had not entered my main quarters, as I would have smelt him earlier and could already have been on his path. Never mind that now. Decision made, I quickly gear up, force down a light breakfast and some water and set out.

*

*The other guy wakes, after a few days out cold, to a raging headache, the driest mouth he's ever experienced and a sound, both familiar and unfamiliar, that he cannot immediately place. The fire that he built for himself when he stumbled into this cave after slogging for what seemed like days, but was likely a few hours, down the barely damp canyon bed, has long gone out, and the cave felt like it must have been cold and damp for days. The cave is set into the wall of the canyon, four feet or so above the ground, and hadn't been easy for him to scramble into in his weakened state, but he'd felt safer at the sight of it than any of the lower down caves, and once again, his instincts have saved him, as he discovers when he feebly sits up, and looks out to the canyon beyond. That sound which he could not immediately identify, was the sound of rapidly rushing water, the surface of which lapped greedily only inches below the floor of his temporary home. Had he chosen one of the lower caves, he would have been submerged, and likely drowned in his drug addled state.*

*Upon entering the cave, that unknown length of time before, he had quickly built and lit a fire, swallowed several antibiotic tablets and anti-inflammatories, and drawn up a generous dose of morphine, before wrapping himself in that thick fur blanket and drifting into the deep, dreamless sleep of the unconscious.*

*It must have rained prodigiously in that time. He is unsure how much time has passed. A couple of days at least, judging by his thirst. He gulps down the remaining water in the large flask he stole from the whore and crawls to the edge of the cave to refill it, dropping in half a tablet to purify it. His fever has broken and he feels hungry for the first time in many days, which is a good sign indeed. While he waits for his water to be ready, he wolfs down half of his food supplies, barely stopping to breathe, so ravenous is his need. When his hunger is sated, he unwraps his mangled arm to inspect the damage.*

*And damaged it is. The redness and swelling is significantly reduced, but for all the infection has improved, the limb is clearly useless. He cannot move a single finger, in fact, there is no* movement below the elbow at all. He can make the limb flop, but that is all. It is nothing more than a hunk of dead meat, attached to that which is living by bone and a few scraps of flesh. He clumsily builds another fire from the ample driftwood in the cave and sits back for a while, enjoying the heat and turning over his new problem in his mind. He had hoped, somewhat foolishly, that were he able to combat the infection, the arm might be of some use still, but it is clear that the tendons, ligaments, nerves and muscles that served to operate his arm, are destroyed beyond repair.

The other guy sighs, almost wistfully. At least he was able to put down the beast that did the damage. He adds more fuel to his fire, understanding now what must be done. He has ample morphine remaining, and more antibiotics. He has the machete, which credit to the whore, has been kept wickedly sharp. No sense in delaying the inevitable. He builds the fire as much as he can over the next hour, and places the machete in its depths, heating the blade as much as possible, and swallows a few more painkillers and antibiotics with his purified water, before refilling the flask once more. He draws up another shot of morphine ready, and places the needle and syringe close at hand.

He removes his belt and ties a tight tourniquet, just above the elbow. He has approximately three inches of flesh and bone unharmed below the elbow, which he hopes to preserve. He waits a few moments, gathering his courage, and allowing his flesh to become numb from the lack of circulation, then takes his own knife to hand. He begins to cut through the flesh, taking it as far down to the bone as he can, but within a few seconds he is gasping and sweating, my god is he crying? Yes, there are tears mingling with the sweat on his face, his efforts to numb himself seem worth nothing, and what started as finessed strokes deteriorates swiftly into frenzied hacking. Blood is flowing copiously despite his best efforts with the tourniquet, and his fingers are slipping, the handle of the knife both tacky and slimy, causing him to fumble and slip when handling the knife. He isn't even halfway around his arm yet, and he must stop, panting and mewling, his breath rasping in and *out, the knife slipping from his grasp and clattering on the rocky base of the cave.*

*His vision is swimming, darkening at the edges and he closes his eyes for a moment, hoping to centre himself, take a breath, collect his strength and start again, but his world tilts sideways. Before he can even open his eyes again his face has collided with the floor, mashing his lips against his teeth and splintering his nose, so now blood is pouring from his face as well as his arm. He lays like that, on the floor, dust and dirt sucked into his mouth and mingling with the blood on his tongue, and for a* moment, just for a moment, *he entertains the notion of stopping, just stopping, and allowing the world he knows to end, and the darkness to win. His eyes drift closed and he's so very cold, and yet somehow warm at the same time, and a feeling of contentment blooms behind his closed eyes, spreading and consuming from within.*

*No! NO! A bolt of adrenaline rips through him and he forces himself upright again, staring blearily at his arm, or what remains of it. He fumbles for his knife and finds he can barely grip the handle. His eyes drift to the machete, blade still buried in the glowing coals, and knows he is running out of time if he is to finish the job successfully. He is bleeding more than he thought he would with the belt acting as a tourniquet, and he must quell this wound before it is too late.*

*He reaches for the machete, and the handle, though wooden and not in the fire itself, blisters his palm instantly on contact and he drops it back into the coals, showering himself with flying shards of flame that seem to burrow beneath his skin like needles. He flails weakly at his shirt when an ember lands there and catches with some force, raising a flame and burning a hole two centimetres in diameter before he is able to quench the flame with his own hand. He smells something sweet, not dissimilar to a juicy whore roasting, and realises it is his own cooked flesh he smells. His stomach rumbles in spite of himself and he has a rare, true moment of clarity upon realising that in spite of all his posturing, and belief that somehow his genitals and ruthlessness make him superior, that he is in fact made out of the same flesh as every woman he has beaten, eaten or raped. Had the thought more time to catch hold, perhaps it would have led him somewhere, because is not the antithesis to all discrimination, the realisation that we are in fact, all the same?*

*But time to catch it did not have, for the other guy steels himself, grabs that handle again and in a single, surprisingly strong and fluid movement, hacks through the remnants of his arm and then presses the blade, steaming as his blood and sweat instantly evaporates, against the bloody, weeping stump.*

\*

I stare at the entrance to the canyon in consternation. Frustration. No, it goes beyond something as simple as frustration. Pure, venomous, *seething,* **boiling** rage. For whether by design or accident, I find that my foe has defied and evaded me, though I have fair certainty as to his rough location. I have tracked him here, by spoor and by smell, sometimes losing the trail but allowing my instincts to guide me and continuing until I picked it up again and within a few hundred meters, just as I knew that the trail leading to Hope was also leading to water, I knew that the trail to the other guy was leading to the canyon proper. And with our recent deluge from the sky, the canyon bed has transformed from that gently burbling trickle that populates it in the summer months, to the furious torrent of white crested floodwater that marks it after a storm of the like we have experienced. The only way I'm getting into that canyon is by trying to seek purchase on the slick rock walls that tower over that rushing tempest, and one slipped finger or toe and Ayla is not more. I might, *might,* be willing to take that risk if I knew for sure where the other guy was, but my heart knows he could be anywhere. This canyon has a multitude of caves inset into its walls, some of which are now below the water line, and that's assuming that he even stayed in the canyon, and hasn't come back out, or been swept away in those waters himself.

Damn him! I swear, colourfully, and launch a vicious kick at a nearby bush, earning myself nothing except a few new scratches and the reinforced awareness that it's rarely helpful to take out your frustration on that which is inanimate, especially when the inanimate can kick back (in its own way). I could wait him out; if the rain settles to a soft drizzle, or abates entirely for a few days, the water level in the canyon will lower and the speed of the water will slow enough for me to safely traverse it. If. But can I even spare a few days, especially for an if or a maybe? I know the answer even as I know that there is no guarantee that a few days respite will give me what I need. The sullen, steel gray clouds pressing down claustrophobically overhead and wet clothing and hair clinging so closely to my skin give me little hope that the rains will stop. Rain as unrelenting as this can make you question what dry clothing and summer warmth even felt like. It's only been a few days but I feel as though I will never be warm and dry again!

I grudgingly turn my back to the canyon and the slippery prey to be found within, and begin trudging back to camp, which I find I no longer call home when I think of it. It had truly become home when Hope was with me. Which just goes to show that home has nothing to do with possessions, or comfort, a sense of ownership or even safety. Home can be found within love. Tears spill over my lids again, mingling with the rain streaking down my face and I don't bother to dash them away. The rain will clean them off.

I find myself, in weaker moments, railing against the injustice of the world, *the universe,* perhaps, furiously screaming into the uncaring, unforgiving nights, the void that surrounds me, that *it isn't fair, goddamit!* Why did I have to lose her as well? Haven't I lost enough? Haven't I *hurt* enough? Why me? **Why must this happen to me?!**

After a little time and more sobbing and wailing, my sense will reassert itself. Of course the universe is unfair. This world and the time leading up to it were the *epitome* of unfair, at least for my gender. I need to let go of any romantic notions that Hope and I were meant to meet, even *destined* to come together, since that requires belief in the notion that all of this pain was also *meant* to happen. This world is cold and callous, chaotic and cruel, and there's no benefit to wondering why that is, only in trying to figure out how to live in it without ending up on some man's dinner table, bed, or both, served up as a sacrifice to his or their satiable lusts. The time of the philosophers, thinkers and artists is long past. This is the time of the warrior, the beast and the slave. I know which one I want to be.

I force my heart to harden and wipe my face, symbolic as the gesture may be with the rain that instantly wets it again. No more tears. No more wailing, sobbing, or railing against the injustice. Hope is gone, and I must move on.

*

Twelve hours after I return to the camp and begin packing my saddlebags and preparing myself for the journey ahead, I am straddling my loaded bike near the tree-line and examining the facade for any weaknesses. I wear my full kit as I'd planned, excepting the boot mods which are in the saddlebags along with the rest of my supplies. The rain has, mercifully, ceased for the moment and a weak sun wrestles with thick cloud cover, punching small spotlights and reaching out with trembling fingers to caress the sticky mud and glistening leaves that carpet the clearing that I think of as my front yard.

I've dragged in my water heater, charging battery packs and the various pieces of equipment that had been scattered across the ground, and placed the camouflaging screens. From this distance, with my eyesight, it is clear that the screens are a ruse. I try to imagine what it would have looked like with my prior vision and come up short. I squint my eyes, trying to blur my vision, but only bring the area I examine into sharper focus.

Balls. I sigh. There's nothing to be done, not really. These screens have protected my camp for many years. Or perhaps they haven't and it is simply that no one ever stumbled across it before Shit for Brains. I'll never be sure, but I know I didn't let it stop me leaving before. So I shouldn't now. Besides, the person most likely to return here is the other guy, since he already knows the exact location and what treasures I hoard. Of course he'll be expecting an extra treasure to be in residence (though I suspect he thinks of me in rather less flattering terms) but at least I can rob him of that satisfaction, not to mention the chance to ambush me. I shall have to be very careful when I take up residence here again.

I press the button to start the engine, which starts as smoothly as a whisper, and with less noise, and set off, riding into the gloomy morning.

# **Chapter Eleven**

*The other guy awakens, not in waves this time, but with a heart-stopping start, as* something *skitters over his face and tears him from his painless slumber. He jolts to a sitting position and is immediately overcome with nausea and dizziness, spraying bile from his mouth in a wave. Unable to keep his equilibrium, he falls face first into the cold, ashen remains of his fire. The thankfully, completely extinguished fire. He inhales reflexively and is rewarded with a lung-full of ash. He rolls away, coughing, spluttering, near enough choking, and clears his airway with an overwhelming sense of,* just in time.

*His vision is spotty as it is and he blinks, hard, a few times, trying to clear what he assumes is ash from his eyes, but to no avail. The dark spots are in his vision he realises, and he lays still and closes his eyes, allowing his heart and breathing to slow, for his body to acclimatise to his life no longer being in danger. He sits up again, propping himself against the cave wall this time, and fumbles for the water bottle that he knows is nearby, his remaining hand grasping blindly until it closes around the cool, smooth metal. He opens his eyes again to remove the cap, and as the cool water slides down his raw, parched throat, those eyes close again, now in ecstasy.*

*He drains the whole bottle and crawls to the cave entrance to refill it, but finds he must now stretch much further to fill the bottle, for the water level has lowered by at least two feet, and is no longer a rushing, deadly tempest. It is passable, not that he considers the possibility of moving on just yet. He drops half a tablet into the water and sits back in his place, pulling his stolen fur blanket tight around him, and allows himself a full minute of rest before the next task of building a new fire, and then of examining his arm, which he has avoided so far with judicious application of simply not looking, and keeping his eyes closed.*

*After a few seconds though he finds he must move, for it is so cold and damp that shivers are wracking his body, and each convulsion sends a bolt of pain up the remnants of his arm, preventing him from relaxing. His teeth chatter, filling his ears with a sound like dice clattering together, and perhaps that's why he doesn't notice the other sound immediately. The sound of...smacking, and small teeth grinding, of flesh tearing and wood and dust being disturbed. Sharp claws skittering over rock floor. The grinding scrape of sharp teeth hitting bone. As he registers the sound and turns his head to it, he is met with the sight of a lizard, too large to be small and yet too small to be large, tearing into his severed arm with relish. He sits for a moment, watching. The lizard hasn't acknowledged him, or fled at his prior movement, so this little chappie has likely not encountered humans in its life, and was simply drawn by the smell of his meat. His fingers are already stripped back to the bone and the lizard presently has his teeth sunk into the meaty flesh that padded the base of his thumb.*

*The machete is fairly close to hand and the other guy leans over to retrieve it, slowly, not wanting to spook the lizard and lose the first fresh meat he will have eaten in what seems like weeks now. The lizard pauses in its mastication, fixing him with a beady eye, and the other guy stills and averts his eyes. It only take a few seconds for the lizard to return to his meal and the other guy slips his fingers around the handle and grips it tightly. He nearly drops it; he had forgotten about the burns he had inflicted on himself in the process of severing his arm. His stomach clenches and his gorge rises as the reality of that hit him all at once, while watching his flesh being consumed by another. He nearly vomits again but manages to avert it, breathing deeply and slowly, swallowing the water and bile in his mouth as it rises.*

*He shuffles a few inches closer to the lizard and stops. The lizard barely flicks an eye at him this time. A few more inches. The lizard doesn't even glance at him when he swings the blade high and chops through its neck and spine. Cold blood flows over his mutilated flesh and when he separates the gore, he finds that the blade is embedded in his palm, the disembodied one. Pulling it free, feeling the metal grind against his bone as he does so, makes his gorge rise again, freeing the acid, water and bile churning in his stomach, and spraying the lizard, the machete and his now defunct limb. He stares at the mess he's made in consternation. He's tempted to hurl the whole, stinking lot into the water and be done with it, but he needs the food and needs the weapon more, so painstakingly, he washes first the lizard and then the machete, groaning as he stretches down with his one hand to sluice them in the running water. His arm he throws away without a second thought, all but a single, clean picked finger bone which he slips into his pocket.*

*He's hungry now, ravenously so, and he builds the fire and quarters the lizard as quickly as his single, burnt limb will wallow, chopping off the chunky long tail as well and setting it aside. He pulls the fur around himself again once the fire is set, waiting impatiently to be able to start roasting the lizard. He takes a long, blissful swallow from the water canister and sets it down, eying the pathetic, bloodied corpse of the lizard, each quarter consisting of a leg and a hunk of meaty body. He picks up the tail and sniffs it. It smells surprisingly pleasant, the blood rich and metallic. He licks the exposed flesh and sucks a few drops of blood from it, before tearing into the tail with gusto. He sucks the raw flesh right from the bones and is soon starting in on the body and legs of the lizard. He washes every other bite down with the slightly bitter river water and relishes every scrap of the animal, picking over each joint until all that's left of the creature is a small heap of jumbled bones.*

*He sits back and lets out a sigh of contentment. The air has warmed now and he lets the blanket slip from his shoulders as an undignified burp rises from within. His stomach is remarkably settled, until it occurs to him that he has just likely consumed his own rotten flesh, and it would all be for nothing, were it not for the return of his indomitable spirit with the filling of his stomach and the quenching of his thirst. He wills his meal to stay down while his thoughts linger on how much he enjoyed the raw meat, the taste, the texture, even the sliminess of it as it crawled down his throat, seeming to need more in the way of swallowing than cooked meat* would. It had never occurred to him to try his food raw before. Even if the guys he was running with at any point didn't have a slave woman on hand, the other guy would always be near the hierarchical top of any group he ran with, and so would never stoop so low as to be responsible for the cooking of the food, a job that they all agreed was a 'bitch's job'.

Within these rabid packs of men would be a strict order, generally dependant on raw power, though sometimes an element of intelligence would come into play. The other guy was smart enough to see the need for power, but also the danger in having too much power. He would settle himself to the right or the left of the man who held the reins, and content himself with guiding his hand and influencing his decisions, while being so far removed from the bottom rung that he never feared being relegated to what they still called the 'kitchen work' or even worse, position of 'bum bitch'. For when the roving men went too long between women to fuck and eat, they would choose a man or a boy to give himself up to the pleasures of the pack, with the promise that when another woman was found they would be relieved of this onerous duty. The other guy had no intention of feeling another man's cock slip up his asshole, or sliding into his mouth, and had in fact killed one of his first packs with his bare hands when it was suggested that he take the role, alerting them to how dangerous he was. All too late for those guys.

So the other guy gets his first taste of cold blood and raw flesh, and wonders if he will enjoy the taste of the whore even more if he eats her raw. He had planned on drawing out the torture so that she would still be alive when he started cooking her. He had even contemplated cooking a body part at a time while she still breathed, and had wondered how long she would survive such an assault before her body gave up and she slid into shock and death. Now he wonders how long she can survive him ripping out chunks of bare flesh with his teeth, and cutting off fingers and toes so he can suck the flesh from them while she watches. He can always cauterise as he goes, he muses, though that might ruin the taste a bit.

*Still, he thinks, there is time. For his bloody stump now requires his attention and he swallows some painkillers before stretching the arm out in front of him and examining the results of his frenzied hacking. The stump oozes a light coloured fluid and is blackened and charred and incredibly sore, but there is no blood and though it is so, so painful to touch, the surrounding flesh is not hot and only slightly swollen. He himself does not feel all that feverish. He smears the stump with antiseptic ointment and wraps it tightly in clean bandages, an action he had failed to complete after the amputation, due to the rapid onset of unconsciousness. Now, he leans back again, and considers his next move. It seems wise to stay at least a few days, and allow the stump to heal more before he can present a challenge of any sort to the whore, but with the water in the canyon this much lower, perhaps some reconnaissance would be wise. He had after all observed her for some time without her realising it before he killed the beast. His binoculars made it with him somehow, though he doesn't recall how he kept them to hand after the confrontation with the beast. No matter. He will go tomorrow. Until then, more sleep is in order to promote healing, and he loads up on another shot of morphine, a smile smeared across his features as he drifts away.*

\*

I set the bike on its stand and swing my leg off in an arc, stretching my back, shoulders and spine with pleasure and rolling out my joints. I've been riding for several hours straight, my bike only achieving fifteen miles an hour at best on most of the roads I've traversed, and largely less than that. There are always a multitude of roadblocks to challenge my path, abandoned cars for the most part, overturned signs and poles, piles and mounds of collapsed concrete from ruined buildings, road blocks and structures that at one time must have divided roads and controlled traffic. The rain of the previous few days has downed many trees and turned many stretches of road into a veritable morass, requiring me to go out of my way to find firmer road or on several occasions, to dismount and push the bike, to avoid getting bogged so far down as to be unable to move. For a fleeting moment, I find myself regretting not bringing a truck, then shake my head. With a truck I'd be constantly having to clear the roads rather than weaving in and out through obstacles. My way is still quicker, even if it is less comfortable.

I estimate that I'm within a few miles of the first location I plan to check, a small backwater hospital that I've near enough cleared out by myself. If I get no luck there, there is a small clinic another fifty miles or so west of there. I should be able to check them both in a day. As much as I've cleared much of the stockpile at my first location, I was never looking for this medication and there's a reasonable chance that few people in this world are either, so if they stocked it, it may well still be there. I've decided to stop for the night at a small trailer, set a few hundred meters back from the road, that I spied when a blinding flash of light escaped through the clouds and I reflexively turned my face away at the perfect moment to spot the structure. It is well screened by shrubbery and trees and I doubt many people without my excellent eyesight would be able to spot it from the road. After all, I've travelled this way myself many times and never come across it before. Which just goes to show that you should never assume anything.

I've positioned the bike so that it is completely screened by the shrubbery, and decide to investigate the trailer before unpacking any of my supplies. I loosen the knife and axe in their sheathes out of habit, but don't draw my bow or nock an arrow, heading straight for the door of the trailer, which does cover the entrance despite it hanging crookedly on its hinges. I fail to notice the fresh footprints in the mud until I'm reaching for the handle, and as I halt the movement of my feet and pull my hand back to reach for a weapon, the door bursts open in a powerful movement, the handle hits me square in the solar plexus and before I've registered what has happened, I am on back, barely able to breathe, and fighting down nausea.

Before I can even draw a full breath there is a knee planted in my chest, a Smith and Wesson pointed in my face, and my capacity for breathing is reduced to zero as any air remaining in my lungs is forced out. I try to draw air in and fail. My vision begins to darken around the edges and narrows to a pinprick, until my whole world consists of gleaming metal and a great, yawning black hole. The barrel disappears and I catch a glimpse of matted blonde hair, greying beard shot through with red and silver and what seems like acres of old, cracked leather, before blinding pain erupts from my temple and across my right eye. The blow disorients me, but doesn't knock me out, which must be what this guy is expecting as almost immediately the weight is lifted from my chest and I hear the scuffle of boots as he stands beside me. I play quiet for now as my lungs finally expand and fill with air. I feel the splatter of warm spittle across my cheek and the slow, viscous drip of his saliva off my nose, before I hear  those boots move away from me, in the direction of my bike.

When I hear him unbuckling my saddlebags I pull my knees to my chest, roll forward and crouch in one fluid movement. My face throbs where he whipped me with the pistol and my eye is already swelling, restricting my vision. Some hot fluid is creeping down my cheek and leaking from my injured eye, but I force this from my mind and focus on the brute pawing through my supplies. He hasn't heard me rise from the ground and clearly doesn't consider me to be a threat, and why would he? Women are for sustenance and satisfaction in this age. He probably hasn't met a woman who could threaten him in decades, if ever.

I examine him closely for a few seconds, observing how he moves. He turns his entire head when looking at things to his left, but not when looking to his right. Blind in one eye perhaps, or severely impaired? I creep around to his left, pondering how best to take him down. He might hear me unstrapping the bow and nocking an arrow. Same with the blowgun and darts. He's around six foot two and looks like he was once built like a tank, judging by the breadth of his shoulders, but the way his clothes hang loosely suggest he has lost a lot of his power and bulk. He holds his left leg stiffly in comparison to his right, suggesting an injury there too. I unsheathe my bowie knife and straighten my body some, so I'm no longer crouched but my knees are still bent, legs parted to just wider than shoulder height, and continue circling to his left, closing the distance between us.

Just as I am positioned to be able to leap forward and bury the blade in his cervical spine, my toe catches a pebble and dislodges it, sending a scatter of earth in his direction. His head whips around, his shoulders just behind, and yes, I was right. Where his left eye once was there is now a gnarled crater of scar tissue, knotted flesh and greyish pink whorls of damaged skin extending out from the site of the injury in a fashion that is almost concentrical. I stare at it for a split second longer than I should have, giving him time to turn his body fully to face me.

I notice, almost idly that he drags the toes of his left foot as he turns. His right hand, still holding the gun, rises to meet me, almost as though in slow motion. Either he moves slowly or my perceptions are faster than they once were, as I have time to observe that the safety is engaged and his finger is not yet curled around the trigger, before I surge forward, pushing from the balls of my feet, and slam the heel of my left hand into the meat below his right shoulder, straightening my arm and bracing just before impact. The shock of the movement stops him in his tracks and before he can recover my right hand has gripped his wrist, twisting it around, while my left has braced behind his shoulder, pushing him towards the ground and disabling him before he has a chance to recover.

I bring up my right leg, bending sharply at the knee and as I let go of his shoulder, my foot is positioned at his elbow. I stamp down with all of my force, pulling back on his wrist at the same time and am rewarded with a sharp crack, the tearing sound of rending muscle and a scream that is utterly feminine in pitch and tone, as I give him an elbow that is now effectively double jointed. I palm his gun as his fingers go limp and he drops to the ground, clutching his arm to his chest and rolling and writhing in agony.

Tears are pouring from his good eye and his face is contorted in what must be sheer, white hot pain. I examine the gun, almost casually, admiring the chunky grip and sleek yet aggressive lines of the barrel.

When he stops writhing and howling long enough to open his eye and look at me, he finds himself staring down the barrel of his own gun, as I did only minutes before. I wait long enough for the fear to register in his eye, for the gravity of the situation to trickle through to his brain, for him to understand, *truly understand*, that he is the powerless one. The rain begins to patter, softly at first and then more heavily, mingling with the sticky blood on my face and darkening the aged denim of his jeans. Not quickly enough though, for me to miss the spreading darkness from his crotch, as his bladder let go. He whimpers as my eyes rise, slowly, to meet his own.

"Please…please...oh God please just..." His words trail off into nothing as I cock my head and continue to stare into his eye, unblinking, my face showing nothing.

"God is a construct created by men to control those they placed beneath them," I reply, quoting my mother and speaking so softly that my words might have been lost in the wind that has begun to rise. Loose strands of hair whip across my face, sodden now, stinging as they make contact with my throbbing temple and the split skin of my eyebrow, but I don't flinch, or move, or even blink.

"Just please…oh God please I don't know what to say…I'm sorry ok, please God I'm sorry!" He is sobbing now, almost choking on his breath. I doubt he has registered my words at all. I wonder how I must look to him. A young, blonde woman, slender almost to the point of emaciation now. I probably look like a harsh wind would be the death of me. Instead I now tower over him and am the agent of his destruction. Does he see a woman, or a demon?

I crouch over him and plant my spiked knee in the flesh of his crotch. I imagine that I can feel his balls trying to crawl back inside his body as he shrieks at me, trying to push himself away from me by digging his heels into the ground and pushing. I am filled, not with rage, not even with anger, but with a cold sense of purpose. Of *power.* In this moment, I'm the closest thing to a God he'll ever experience, for is his life, his pain, his *suffering,* not held in my hands? He swipes at my face with his good hand, batting at me ineffectually, and I return the favour, pistol whipping him across his cheekbone. The skin splits in two, spraying me with hot blood and his head snaps to one side, his jaw rigid, a scream erupting through the clenched teeth, and I put a round through his left shoulder. The arm flops as he tries to move it and his eye finds mine again, burning with fear, shame and *impotence,* as I have rendered him so. He is babbling at me now, nonsensical with pain and terror, drool bubbling at his lips and sliding down his cheeks, mixing with the blood, tears and rain already there. I lean closer, close enough to feel drops of saliva pepper my face, to smell the canned meat of his last meal and the grease in his matted hair.

"The only God that concerns you now, little man, is me. Pray to your God for mercy."

He chokes a little and starts babbling again, a mixture of pleases and oh Gods that displease me.

"*Pray. To. **Me**.*"

His eye widens, his words fail him and his mouth hangs open. I slide the barrel into his open mouth and see in his eye what I've been waiting for. The departure of hope. The acceptance of fate. His face relaxes and his eye drifts closed as I pull the trigger and blast the grey matter that made up this guy's entire life across a three meter radius.

Later that night, as I curl up on the lumpy cushions that served as his bed, wrapped in my sleeping bag, my mind lingers on that moment. On the cold clarity I felt looking down on the man I was about to kill. The sharp pleasure that his fear brought me. The power that surged through me, that felt to almost singe me when I saw him accept his fate and give himself up to me. The powerful, almost sexual pleasure that gripped me as I pulled the trigger. A harder woman indeed I have become.

# Chapter Twelve

*Let our gaze now withdraw, move back, move **up**, and expand. Let us move away from the woman, young yet old, grappling with her new self, and relishing pain in a new and frightening way. Let us slip back from the man, old in both flesh and spirit, who is swiftly accepting his altered form and adapting to maximise his deadly potential, even in his weakened state. Let us sweep down the canyon, past the mouth, away from the woman's camp and the man's covert foxhole. Let us follow the curve of the river, a raging tempest only two days before, now still a healthy flow but one far less deadly in its nature.*

*We need only follow the water a few miles past the canyon mouth, to be brought to our point of interest, and our vision narrows, focuses and homes in to observe a great, hulking pile of fur covered flesh. Fur that appears at first glance to be a muddied brown and black, but when the sun breaks through the pregnant clouds and caresses that fur with a tentative touch, it highlights shades of gold and ochre, amber and bronze, molten copper and warm honey, that seem like they should not exist in nature.*

*At first glance it would seem that this hulking mass has simply washed up on the bank of the river, but a closer inspection will show that its path was blocked by a large chunk of rock, initially submerged and gradually exposed as the water level lowers with the lessening rain. Its body is wrapped almost completely around the rock so that even with the decreased water height, the obstacle to its continued travel is barely visible. But an obstacle it is, for instead of continuing along its path, the pile remains where it is, fur being gradually exposed and slowly drying in the weak snatches of sunlight.*

*Though the heap of fur, flesh and bone, has by all accounts been dead these several days past, there is little to indicate this state of being to us, the casual observer. The flesh beneath the pelt is still curiously plump with no signs of wastage, nor the bloated belly of death. The eye sockets are not yet sunken, nor does the jaw hang agape in the yawn of the departed. No maggots are visible in the open wound atop the fine skull, and no flies buzz and bumble, or rub their front legs together in glee at the scent of dead and rotten flesh. And yet, there is that wound, gaping and hideous, a crater in its skull, an injury that no man or beast could survive. The wound remains.*

\*

I stretch and wriggle in the warm cocoon of my sleeping bag, eyes still closed against the probing, piercing light of early morning. My nostrils are filled with the musty scent of old trailer and the greasy stink of unwashed man, but it beats sleeping on the ground. I stretch out an experimental arm and immediately withdraw to my nest. The air is colder than I expected and I hunker down further, savouring the comfort and warmth for a few moments more, before forcing myself to face the day. I find myself more tired than I expected from the exertions of the prior day, despite the physical enhancements Hope has wrought in me. I must have lost a lot of conditioning during my convalescence and period of grief. I certainly lost a few kilos more than I could afford.

My hand drifts down, almost unconsciously, to scratch an itch behind my knee. Instead of abating, the itch intensifies, until I'm all but tearing at my skin. As though awakening every inch of my skin, I find myself scratching my arms, legs, back, belly, every part of me that I can reach. I pull my hands out of the sleeping bag and there is blood and skin clotted beneath my nails and on my fingertips. I feel a tell-tale tickle streak across my collarbone and slap the area, hard, and pull my hand back. Bedbugs! Of course. Why wouldn't they survive the apocalypse? They can survive pretty much anything else. I throw myself out of my sleeping bag and hastily toss my detached saddlebags out the door. Hopefully the little bastards focused on my living flesh and have yet to infest my supplies.

As I strip my clothes and inspect them and my skin for errant bugs, I wrathfully recall the great infestation of 2030 that nearly led to my father burning our modest home to the ground. We battled those things for months, and even after the application of some hideously caustic chemicals which burned through several layers of skin and felt like inhaling fibreglass, we still found bugs on many occasions over the coming years. I had gotten into the habit of meticulously checking my bed and bedclothes on a nightly basis, but this habit was long forgotten by this time. An oversight, it would seem.

I inspect every seam of my clothing and every nook and cranny on my person and after meticulous searching which takes over an hour, I am as satisfied as I can be that I am free of these foul creatures. Only then do I make a breakfast out of the cans of meat and fruit that this guy had hoarded in his ramshackle trailer. He had little else of worth to me, and I have no intention of returning to the trailer to look for more.

After loading up my saddlebags, before setting off, I amble around the back of the trailer for a final, morbid look at the body of the man I put down yesterday. I didn't bother to dig him a grave; he wasn't worth the expenditure of energy. I expect to find his corpse where I left it, after dragging him out of sight by his heels, and pull up short when I round the trailer. His body is still there all right, but I'm not sure I would call it a singular item anymore. *Something* tore him apart in the night, something *big*. He is completely dismembered, intestines and viscera spread across a four meter radius, and as far as I can tell, he's missing his head. I kneel next to a mangled arm and use a small stick to gingerly part the rent cloth and get a better look at the wound. Most of the limb is torn to shreds but I can clearly make out three, deep, rivets in the flesh. Claws? Or teeth? I can't imagine any animal currently living that could do this kind of damage, not in my arid part of the country. Of course there used to exist mammals that could tear a man limb from limb, but even then, not in this part of the world. I can't imagine even a cougar would be able to do this, were they not presumably all but extinct now, and if I recall correctly, they did not hunt like *this*. So wasteful. So...*garish.*

My skin prickles as gooseflesh pimple, and the hair rises on the back of my neck. I may not know what caused this, but I know that I don't want to meet it. My eyes drift to the dusty trailer, sagging and creaking, all but falling down, and despite the bedbugs, I am so, *so* grateful for it. Who knows what would have become of me had I slept on the ground last night? I turn from the mass of gore and in my hurry to leave the horror behind, I fail to notice the picked clean jumble of human bones mixed in with those of the fresh remains.

*

*The other guy creeps along, picking his way through mud and soggy brush, cursing the thorns that tear his skin and the struggle to protect himself with only one working hand while holding on to his meagre supplies. And the binoculars. Must hold on to the binoculars. He was already soaked through up to the knees from wading through the water in the canyon, but the squelch of the mud and prick of the thorns adds an extra layer of indignity to the already uncomfortable task. The sun is out today, albeit weakly, and steam gently rises from the moist leaves and grass, mingling with the midges that seem to rise from nowhere as soon as the pattering of rain ceased. The other guy finds himself increasingly discomfited by the simple inability to slap away the bugs that cluster thickly around his hairline and nostrils. He snorts and puffs, trying to dislodge the little bastards, but achieves only the expulsion of a great wad of mucus, which hangs maddeningly from his chin. He sets down the binoculars on a handy rock and wipes his face with his remaining hand.*

*He is nearly to his prior vantage point and so he pushes on after a few cursory swipes to remove the midges, a pointless endeavour it would seem given the dozens more that immediately flock to take the place of those now smeared across his brow and upper lip. A few dozen meters more and he is in his prior foxhole and settling the binoculars in place. A surge of adrenaline floods his body, sending a bolt of pain through his severed arm, when he sees...nothing? No camp, no whore, no equipment. It looks like the overgrown side of a cliff! He glances around himself, placing the landmarks he recalls. He looks down into the hollow in which his knees rest. He is definitely in the right place. How can an entire camp disappear in the space of a few days?*

*He sits back on his heels and mulls it over, then peers through the binoculars again. There's no way those inset caves have gone anywhere, so they must be hidden, and as that thought slides across his mind, his perspective shifts, akin to those pictures in magazines bought for him as a child. Those pictures that looked like an ordinary scenery, until you looked and looked and looked and suddenly, clear as day, you see there was a tiger in the middle of the picture all along. Once you see it, you never understand how you did* not *see it in the first place. It becomes immediately apparent that the overgrown cliffside is in fact a set of camouflaging screens, and despite himself, he feels a grudging sort of respect rise for the whore. Perhaps she has survived this long by more than just the efforts of the beast he slaughtered.*

*Is she in the caves, hidden behind those screens? The place looks abandoned; none of the equipment previously scattered about is visible. It's possible that she is waiting, to ambush him or perhaps another. He decides to wait and watch for some hours. He finds himself in no rush, after all.*

\*

I make pretty decent time to the little hospital, trying very hard the whole way to not think about the scene I just departed. As widespread and savage as the carnage was, there still felt as though there was something almost *deliberate* about the placement of the dismembered parts, and I wonder had I stayed to examine the remains longer, if I might have noticed a pattern.

The last time I came I wedged cardboard into the lock of one of the rear fire entrances, thinking to save myself a more conspicuous entry through the smashed in front glass doors. I remember thinking those doors were magical when I first came across them, in labour thirteen years ago, and being almost embarrassed to find out the technology was so old hat as to be boring. At least a traditional door has the advantage of being functional without power. At first and probably second glance, the fire door looks closed and locked, but when I sidle closer, watching my surroundings warily, I see my little tab poking out of the frame and give it a pull. As I'd hoped, the door swung open with ease and little noise, leading me into a dark stairwell interspersed with narrow shafts of light from the small window on each floor.

The room I'm aiming for is on the first floor, the pharmacy past the first of many eerie, empty wards filling the abandoned building. I have a small, hand wound torch that I use for occasions like this and I pull it out and click it on out of sheer habit before I remember that I have no need for torches anymore, at least not so far on my journey. It seems to be that any light, no matter how small, is enough light now.

I creep up the silent stairwell and peer around the door leading me into the first floor. My sharp eyes detect no movement and I hear nothing to worry me, just a few quiet scurries and rustles that sound like insects and small lizards. Slipping through I work my way down the corridor, checking each empty room I pass to ensure that they are in fact empty, and then work my way through the remaining boxes and bottles littering the small pharmacy. There is little left here, so the search doesn't take long. No luck.

I'm working my way back down the corridor, more swiftly than when I came through, when a dust encrusted sign near the stairwell catches my attention. I see the word pharmacy and rub the sign clear with a handful of scattered papers. The pharmacy it is signposting to me is of course the one I have just checked, but another word catches my roving eye. Maternity and OBGYN. I know the meaning of these words from my well thumbed copy of Gray's Anatomy and I wonder if a specialised department might have their own pharmacy, not advertised to the public.

Happy with that logic, I work my way up to the next floor and open the door, to be faced, yet again, with the barrel of a fucking gun. A smaller gun this time, more of the peashooter variety but peashooter or not, at this range it'll give me plenty of trouble. I brace myself for an attack that never comes, and realise to my astonishment that this gun is wielded by another woman. Though the small hand holding the gun with a white knuckled death grip is shaking, the dark eyes almost directly behind could be made from tempered steel. Those eyes tell me that she will have no trouble pulling that trigger, though why she has yet to do so is unclear.

I hold my hands up before me in the universal gesture of peace and try for a smile, not moving an inch forwards or backwards. As she considers me I become aware of what I can only describe as a *pulsing* sensation in my head, as though someone is probing my brain with ghostly fingers. It feels...curious. And afraid. That fear hits me and threatens to envelope me, all the while knowing that that fear is not my own. This woman however may be willing to kill me but she doesn't *want* to, and that makes her about as close to a friend as you get in this world we live in. I take a few deep breaths and try to concentrate. Just as I am able to read this woman's base intent, I also know that it's not her fingers poking around in my head.

"I...er...come in peace?" I try for the smile again and am met with a locked jaw and unflinching onyx eyes. She's having none of it. Can't exactly blame her. I've hardly made it a policy to be friendly to strangers this past decade.

"What do you want?" Straight to the point. I like it. Her voice is husky, deeper than I expected. A little rough around the edges but deep enough that you want to swim in it. I kinda like that too.

"I'm looking for a medicine, that's all. It wasn't downstairs so I was hoping the maternity pharmacy might have it." I have no idea if there is actually a maternity pharmacy or not but I want her to know I'm here for a singular purpose, and not just roving around.

The woman stares at me for an uncomfortably long time, deliberating. I spend the time taking her in and I have to say, I like what I see. Wild, thick black hair, barely constrained by a hairband, liquid dark eyes and a pert, almost petulant mouth. She is small, smaller than me by a few inches, and petite. Her hair seems to make up at least half of her body mass. Her skin is criss crossed with fine scars, what I can see of it, but that skin still looks silky soft and inviting. I want to touch her. I feel a sensation so unfamiliar it takes me a moment to even place it. A tug of lust, a flash of heat. Am I feeling desire for this woman? I can see the bubbled scar tissue creeping up her neck over her collar, but even this does not detract from her appeal.

She is still contemplating me and a single word arrives, unannounced in my mind. *Safe.* I blink, even more confused and even more sure that that did not come from the woman standing before me.

"What medicine are you looking for?" The woman has relaxed, just a touch, not lowering the gun but also not gripping it so urgently. She is taking me in too, clearly intrigued by my eyes but trying not to show it. Her eyes note the fresh bruising on my face, my ample weaponry, my clothing.

"Mifepristone."

"Speak English."

"It's er...I...er...well it's an abortion medication."

A shade of pity and something else, an emotion I can't quite place, crosses her eyes and she looks away from me, to the floor. She probably thinks the recent bruising and my hunt are connected. She likely can't see the fading, yellowed bruises that still dot my skin in the dim light that trickles into the hallway.

She lowers the gun a few inches and beckons for me to come in front of her, pointing me to my place.

"The pharmacy is at the end of this hall. I'm going to follow you, and my gun will be pointed at your head the whole time. Do you understand me?" Her voice cracked a little on the last syllable and I don't know why or how, but that little break sends warm shivers down my spine. I could listen to that voice for days on end. I nod my assent and start walking, slowly and deliberately and within a few paces I feel that pulsing again, stronger now, and calmer, and this time I barely feel any fear at all.

"Is there someone else here, with you?" I ask, without breaking stride and hear the steps behind me instantly come to a halt and the cocking of the gun behind my head.

"Get out." That voice is considerably less erotic with the emphasis of genuine threat behind it. I stop and turn to face her, noting the narrowed eyes, furrowed brow and snarling upturn to that mouth, no longer petulant, now pissed off and yes, frightened. I can feel the fear rolling off her in waves, but not fear of me directly. There's definitely someone here and it's someone she cares very deeply for.

"I'm not going to do anything or hurt anyone, I swear." I keep my tone even and my voice calm.

"No, I know. You're either going to leave with my boot up your ass or a bullet in your skull. I'm not fucking around. Get out of here, now!"

"Ok. Ok. I'll go, if that's what you want. No problem." I sidle around her and feel those fingers caressing my brain again as I slip back through the stairwell door, once more curious and I think, regretful, that I am leaving. I waste no time in firing up my bike though, and setting off to my next destination. She was serious about putting a bullet in my head and I'm pretty sure she'd considered doing it even if I left without a fuss. I gave one last look over my shoulder before I lift my feet and see a flash of dark hair darting back from the window, too low to have been my mystery gunslinger. I try to recall the feeling of *pushing* myself out when communicating in my way with Hope, and try to push the words *sorry* and *goodbye*. I wait a moment and twist the throttle, as the word *goodbye* arrives in my mind.

# Chapter Thirteen

"Fuck! Goddamn fucking shitfire fucking damn it all to *hell*!" I stand before the gutted remains of what was once the clinic that might have held my salvation, so ragingly furious that my mouth is filled with the taste of metal, and before I even realise it, I've pulled out a clump of my own hair. I'm beating at the ground like a child in the midst of a temper tantrum, and the mental image of how absurd I must look is immediately sobering. I force my fists to relax and brush the dust off my knuckles, massaging them and opening my fingers, allowing several strands of blonde hair to float to the ground. My knuckles are grazed and already slightly swollen. Foolish. I don't need to add to my injuries. I've only been out two days and I already have a shiner and split skin across my temple from my encounter with the one eyed bandit yesterday.

I force myself to breathe more slowly and close my eyes, breathing in through my nose and out through my mouth, willing my heart rate to slow and the adrenaline to stop flooding my veins in lancing waves. Even had the clinic been intact, I knew that it may not have held the medicine I need. Anger won't achieve anything.

I can repeat the words to myself all I want but as it turns out I can't control my responses anymore than I can control those of others. I may not be beating the ground in impotent rage, but as soon as my eyelids snap open and focus again on the burnt out husk that sprawls before me, I can *feel* my blood pressure rise. My pulse throbs in my ears and my lower left lid twitches quite violently. I think the wanton waste infuriates me as much as the potential destruction of what I need. I was last here only nine months ago to restock, and there was still a decent supply of medicines, bandages and the like here then. I have never taken trucks out on supply runs, preferring the stealth that the bike affords me when out of the park, and so have never fully cleared the stockpile here.

I wonder if the shitbags that torched the place cleared out the supplies first, or if they were just burning for fun. I sit back on my heels and contemplate the prudence of investigating the remains. The destruction appears fairly complete from my vantage point, but I can only see the front few rooms, and the building was fairly spacious. The main storeroom was located close to the rear. There's a chance, albeit a slim one, that there may be intact supplies remaining.

I circle the building first, trying to gauge the extent of the internal damage, hoping to get a view of the storeroom in question, but no luck. The rear of the building seems considerably less damaged though, there being no gaping holes in the walls. The whole building may not have been gutted after all. I jog lightly back to the bike, and consider if I should take anything with me. I'm wearing my gear and most of my weaponry, as planned, and consider removing some, but decide against it. If this brutal world has taught me anything, it has taught me to always be prepared to defend myself. I clip a full water bottle to my belt and tie a length of rope around my waist. I didn't bring any digging tools. Seemed unnecessary when I was planning this.

At least getting in isn't a challenge, since all that remains of the door is ash and the odd stump of charred wood. I step over the threshold and pick my way over and around the debris clustering the floor. The air seems thick with soot and is harsh even to my dust hardened lungs. I pull my snood up over my nose and continue on, past the collapsed desk that once greeted patients and gently push at the door behind, which opens to the corridor which leads to the storeroom and clinic rooms. The door doesn't budge. I push harder, bracing my legs and shoving forward with the heels of my hands. No dice.

This is the only route to the back of house, and it feels thoroughly jammed, but I have no intention of giving up just yet. I step back a pace and kick hard with heel, sending a bone jarring jolt through my pelvis and spine, but I feel a miniscule shift in the positioning of the door. I kick again and feel another small shift, but the movement is little for the expenditure of energy, so I switch to ramming with my shoulder. It hurts more than the kick but I'm rewarded with a visible gap and a shrieking groan as the door shifts inwards by a five or six inches. I stop for a moment and massage my aching shoulder. Strong and agile I may be, but I'm not built to be a battering ram. I hurl myself at the door again and my stomach lurches as the whole door splinters down the middle and I fall straight through.

As I lay on the filthy remnants of what I think was garish green linoleum, breathing in soot and ash despite my efforts with the snood, I become aware of a harsh, needling pain in the flesh of my right upper arm. I roll onto my back and crane my neck to better see the injury, and am met with the sight of a large, jagged wooden splinter piercing my flesh. I barely have time to metaphorically roll my eyes at my bad luck before I become aware of the widening cracks in the plaster of the ceiling above me, the shifting of the surface beneath me, and with a rending sound that evokes genuine terror within me, I am falling.

*

*While Ayla lies unconscious, and the other guy waits and watches, we return to our hulking lump of fur and flesh and observe curious things indeed. Little would appear to have changed since our last visit, until we examine again that gaping wound and find that there is no wound, at least none we can see beneath the thick fur once again carpeting the great skull.*

*As we ourselves watch, and wait, we might observe a twitch of an ear and a jerk of a leg. If we look more closely, we can see razor sharp claws extending and retracting, almost as though convulsing. If we were close enough to risk being scored by those same claws, we might be able to see the rise and fall of a chest, sharp and erratic at first, but growing steadily deeper and more even.*

*We might in fact be able to hear the faintest thrum, a bass note so deep that at first you can only feel it in your chest, vibrating and pulsing. As the rising and falling of that broad chest becomes deeper and more pronounced, so does that reverberating note, until it seems to be rolling in from all sides, rather than emanating from a single source. As the growl reaches its crescendo, the beast leaps to its feet in one fluid movement and spins in a circle, snapping furiously at the air and its surroundings and growling so loudly that were we physically present, we might have to cover our ears.*

*Once it is clear that there is no present danger, the beast stops and looks around itself in a manner that can only be described as bewildered. It pads over to a few trees and rocks, familiarising itself with the scent of its surroundings and with a movement so swift as to be almost invisible, she darts behind a tree and snaps a small lizard up in its jaws, consuming it in one, crunchy, bite. The hunger now upon her, the beast dashes off into the trees, stopping every few dozen meters to sate the raging hunger that consumes the very fibre of her being. The beast has no memories of a woman named Ayla.*

\*

*The other guy stamps his feet and jumps on the spot a few times, trying to encourage the blood to flow into his freezing lower extremities. His stump gives a warning throb but he ignores it. The other guy has always believed the old trope that pain cannot be avoided but suffering is optional. He has been sitting and watching the cave for hours now, and has yet to see any sign of movement. The evening glow has begun to recede and with it his will to continue sitting in the dark, watching and waiting. The beast may be gone, but the other guy finds himself to be wary of the dark now in a way that he never was before. For one thing, if that beast existed, who is to say that other, feral, giant beasts do not also exist in this landscape? For another, the other guy is acutely aware that he did not win that fight based on anything other than pure luck.*

*He shivers as the memories return, images and sensations trickling through his consciousness, stored forever in his limbic* brain. He thought that killing the beast would conquer his fear of it, or at least lessen it, but as it turns out, fear and its memory are nefarious creatures. Once it has its hooks in you, tearing it out is nigh on impossible. A survival mechanism no doubt, a throwback to those days when humans were the hunted, not the hunters, but one that the other guy finds highly inconvenient, not least because the memories would return to him with frightening and unpredictable frequency. Each time they did, his hand would shake, his vision would narrow, adrenaline would flood his body and his mouth and throat would be instantly drier than sand.

He closes his eyes and knuckles them with his remaining, bunched fist, willing the memories to pass and his heart to slow, but the mind is a fickle thing and tends not to obey its master. He can feel the dampness of the leaves and the slipperiness of the sodden earth beneath his skin as he wakes shivering in his foxhole, certain beyond doubt that the beast is coming for him. As he scrambles to his feet and whips his head around, trying to find the most defensible position, he sees nothing more than the trees that have surrounded him for days. He gropes for the gun tucked into his waistband, his hail mary, last hope and act of desperation. He doesn't know if this beast can be killed with a handgun, but this handgun he knows gives him the best chance that he has.

His Desert Eagle, his most precious possession and certainly his last weapon, holding one final bullet, which the other guy has hoarded for many months now, will finally bark its last, booming cough. The other guy crouches, with his back to a tree, waiting and waiting, until finally, after minutes or hours or maybe even days, that growl rolls through the clearing and jars his very bones. His heart rate spikes, his pulse pounding in his ears and for the life of him, he cannot pinpoint which direction the growl is coming from. It rolls through again, deeper and louder, vibrating in his chest and the other guy spins frantically, desperately trying to gauge which way he should be facing.

His palm is so slick with perspiration he fears he will drop the gun or fumble the shot and he trembles so hard his teeth chatter together, like bone dice rattling in a cup. As suddenly as it came, the growl stops, and all the other guy can hear is his own ragged breathing and racing heartbeats, so fast now he can barely distinguish the individual beats. He waits and waits, trying to hear anything over the echoing in his ears. He feels a strange warmth spreading down his legs and realises he has soiled himself in his fear, an act he has not committed since toddlerhood. Never has he felt fear so intense, so visceral, so primal, not even when the beast was tearing through his arm on that first meeting.

He closes his eyes, knowing that in the murky dark they help him little and perhaps that is what saves him, for he hears the tiniest creak from behind and what may have been the crumpling crunch of a dying leaf. He spins, firing as he does and the power of the great beast meets the trajectory of one of the largest caliber bullets that can be fired from a handgun, bursting the skull like an egg dropped on concrete and showering the tree behind with its contents.

As the memories run their course and the other guy regains his place in time and space, he tries to breathe as deeply and steadily as he can. The beast is dead, the beast is dead, the beast is dead, the words tumbling from his mouth almost unconsciously until his breathing begins to slow and his hand stops shaking. The other guy cannot understand the power of these memories, their ability to transport him back to a place he has left, and make him relive not just the memory, but every shiver of fear and spike of adrenaline he experienced at the time.

He focuses his gaze on the caves, and decides to scope them out. He feels almost certain that were she present, he would have seen some sign of it by now, and starts making his way towards them, hugging the treeline and checking his destination every dozen or so yards with the binoculars. He makes it without incident, and sidles up to the cave that he knew to be her residence. He can't help but admire the screens, an exercise in ingenuity if he has ever seen one, and an endeavour that must have taken months to complete. He examines and lifts the edge closest to him, and is pleased to find the screen rolls back easily enough, revealing in the moonlight a cave that looks to be surprisingly homely.

*He notices the bulbs strung around the room and his brow furrows, his eyes seeking....ah. There. He flips a switch and is transported to nearly a decade before, the last time he saw a light powered by electricity. He traces the wiring to their source. A battery. Solar charged he thinks most likely. He explores a little, collecting himself a meal of dried meat and berries along the way, and hunkers down in the bed in the corner, soft and comfortable with its layers of furs and what he suspects is even a makeshift mattress beneath. He elects against lighting a fire; he finds himself more than warm beneath the piles of furs and after swallowing down his painkillers and antibiotics, the other guy is sleeping within a few seconds, cocooned in warmth and comfort that he hasn't experienced in years.*

\*

I squat on the low stool, hunkering down against the biting wind, taking what shelter I can as I milk Bull in the freezing early morning. Bull is our cow. Father named her. He thinks he's hilarious. I can barely feel my fingers as I palm the teats and draw out the fresh milk, steaming in the morning chill, the movements so routine as to be unconscious. I cough a little. The air feels both dry and sharp in my lungs as I inhale, and I hope fervently that I am not becoming unwell. Even a deadly fever doesn't get you dispensation from work in this house, though my mother would try her best to lighten my load in times of prior illness.

I pat Bull's side, and lean my head against her for a moment, rubbing my hands together to try and warm them before I grasp the heavy bucket and take it back indoors. Bull emits a soft low, snorting slightly as she waits for me to be finished. I pat her again, pushing to my feet, and she lows again, louder this time, in that way she does when overdue to be milked and fluid is straining at her udder. Her hide feels odd under my fingertips, almost ridged or raised in patches. I only have the dimmest of light by which to see, since this chore is so natural for me now I do it entirely by feel, not sight.

"What's the matter my girl?" I murmur, stroking her flank and now she bellows, clearly in pain, and I step back, frightened for the first time of this creature which I only now understand could trample me into a damp puddle if she so desired. The pail is still beneath her and she kicks it over, splattering the yard and my legs with warm milk and I continue stepping backwards, through the gate to her enclosure and latching it. My fingers feel curiously tacky, as though her hide left some sticky residue behind when I touched her. Bull continues bellowing as though she hasn't been milked for days as I retreat to the house, surprised that my mother has yet to come running to the source of the noise, frightened of my father's wrath upon waking.

I open the back door and now my hand is gritty as well as tacky, and I wipe it on my jeans as I step over the threshold and flip the light switch, looking down to see what ails me. I realise simultaneously that my hand is covered with flesh coloured, sticky goo and cow hair, and the floor is thickly coated with black dust, almost reminiscent of coal dust. It is oddly familiar though I'm certain I've seen nothing like it before and I leave in it my footprints as I cross to the kitchen, to speak to my mother and to *wash my hand.* My parent's bedroom door is slightly ajar, an odd thing to find at this time of day when noise must be kept so minimal and I turn the handle to the kitchen with caution and care, crossing the threshold and closing it behind me.

The dust carpets this floor too and again I feel the air biting in my lungs, forcing another barking, hacking cough from me. My feet slither and slide with every step as I cross to the sink and turn the tap. I wash my hands, though I can't seem to entirely remove the sticky film and realise I am alone in the room, where my mother is usually found. I cross back to the door and through again, observing with more unease that my parent's bedroom door is now open several inches, though no light from the hallway seems to creep through. I eyeball the half foot gap, seeming to swallow incoming light, leaving only a gaping maw that feels as though it is staring back at me, and dart into Tilly's room thinking that perhaps my mother is in there, checking on my dear girl.

There is only darkness here too, and dust, and I realise with a start that I haven't heard Bull lowing since I stepped back inside the house. With another jolt that shakes me to my core, I see that Tilly is not in her bed. I dash back out and freeze, for that door is now fully open and can I hear voices from within? Those of Tilly and Mother perhaps? I step towards the door, tentatively, frightened now, more so than I think I have ever been, and yes I can definitely hear Mother and Tilly, muffled as though through several walls or layers of blankets. Though I step closer and closer, that blackness simply yawns, not a shaft of light penetrating the dark, and crossing the threshold is akin to stepping through a thick, black curtain.

Mother lays on the bed, face ruined, chest jerking sharply up and down, hands curved into claws by her side, pain written on every movement and lack thereof, even if I cannot read it on her face, overrun by bubbling flesh. I step towards her, ready to fulfil my duty again, and comfort her in her crossing, but stop myself a foot from the bed, because something is wrong, something is *missing* from this scene. With that thought, I hear the rattle of a phlegm clogged throat behind me and whip around to find my father standing less than two feet from me.

He reaches for me and his mouth falls open in a gaping, yawning maw, his skin ruined too, bubbling and oozing from hairline to jaw. How he can even see me, I do not know, for even his eyes are gone, just pits of pus and blisters and as his hands grasp my arms and shove me backwards, hard, I see the skin of his cheeks begin to part, the skin stretching and splitting like melted cheese. I land on my back with a sharp jolt that knocks the wind out of me and before I can regain my feet, his bulk prevents me from drawing breath. As his fingers grasp and fumble at the waistline of my trousers, seeking the buttons that will give him the access he desires, I turn my face away from his, seeming to disintegrate before my eyes.

Under the bed, there is my Tilly, her tiny hand reaching out to me, strands of her fine hair stuck in the blisters that cover her face and now I understand that it was never Bull I could hear crying out, it was Tilly, wailing in unending agony, begging me to release her from the hell of her affliction but I can neither reach her or even draw a breath before I -

Wake, coughing and spluttering, tears pouring down my face as I try like hell to draw air into my lungs. There is a massive weight on my chest and I desperately push what seems to be a hefty chunk of rafter off my sternum, yet still, I cannot breathe. I roll onto my side and hack and hack, and just as my vision is dimming and I wonder why I couldn't have stayed unconscious if I was only going to wake and die immediately, I expel what feels like a massive clot of jelly from my windpipe and draw a desperate, ragged breath. I cough again and this time I cough until I am retching, choking up more balls of this curious jelly.

The coughing abates, eventually, and I see the balls of jelly are in fact balls of soot and phlegm and recall that I am in the basement of a fire gutted building. Shafts of sunlight pierce the darkness and though I am disoriented by my manner of waking, the angle and warm quality of the light leads me to suspect that several hours have passed since I entered this building. I roll to my feet and twinge as several ribs pointedly remind me of their existence. Nothing feels broken but that was one hell of a fall I made. My sternum is on fire where the chunk of ceiling was resting and when I stretch, many more bruises and sore patches clamour for my attention. I pat my back and find the bow still in place, and remind myself to check it and the arrows for damage when I get myself out of here.

I scope my surroundings and see that my egress should be quite easy, despite the nature of my entry, as there are stairs leading up a few meters back from where I came through the ceiling. I clamber up the stairs, eager to escape the close air of the basement, thankful to find an unlocked and unblocked exit. I open the door and step out with gratitude, finding myself in the very storeroom I sought in the first place. I look around in wonder, pleased with both my first real stroke of luck of the day, and to see that the room is remarkably undamaged, comparative to the rest of the building. My initial instincts were right, even if they did lead to me being part of a building collapse.

I start pawing through the shelves and drawers of bottles, boxes and cartons, seeking the right words...mifepristone...mifepristone. My heart flutters every time I see something beginning with m, and my silly mind starts repeating I spy with my little eye every time I see another medication that isn't the one I seek, as though mocking my own self. Mirtazapine, morphine, melatonin, methadone, metformin, my word, I'd never really realised how many of these bloody things started with an m. I spy with my little eye, methocarbamol, metoclopramide, miralax, mifepristo - Wait! I scramble for the little box, heart thumping, blood rushing in my ears and read the label four times, desperate to ensure my grasping, hopeful mind is not playing tricks on me. It isn't, and I feel the tension inside dissipating and my legs weakening as the adrenaline that had been propping me up departs. I snatch another few boxes of painkillers since I didn't bring any and I now have several more injuries to annoy me, and slip out of the door of the storeroom.

There is a gaping hole in the floor where I went through, and a window to my left. I think I'll try the window before navigating that mess again. Slowly, carefully, I cross the floor, testing every step before placing my weight fully, and make it to the outer wall and window without incident. It unlatches and opens in with ease, and I scramble out, eager to escape the suffocating, sooty air within.

I lean against the wall and begin to laugh, elation that my search is over so soon coursing through me and I choke on the inhale and double over, coughing up more of that impressively black goo, tears cutting a swathe through what I imagine must be an impressively black face too. My windpipe clear, I wipe my face and make my way back to the front of the building, where I find, to my abject misery, that my bike is gone.

# Chapter Fourteen

I sit in the dust in front of the gutted clinic, staring at the tracks left by the apparent motorcade that must have stolen my bike. I'm seeing tracks for at least six vehicles here, which could translate to upwards of thirty people depending on the capacity of those vehicles. Or I could get lucky and have crossed paths with six guys who like to have their own ride. What I am certain of is how badly I want that bike back. The supplies attached to it I have in ample form in the caves, but the bike is invaluable to me. I've yet to see another vehicle since the apocalypse that is powered by batteries and I'm bright enough to know that gasoline will run out, perhaps not tomorrow or even in the next few years, but it certainly will, and the lack of a combustion engine makes the bike gloriously easy to maintain and keep on the road.

The light is dwindling, caressing my sooty arms and legs with golden fingers, highlighting shimmering motes even in the remnants of destruction. I push to my feet. I can't do much about this today. I'll follow the tracks until I find a house or a trailer that will shelter me for the night, and plan out my course tomorrow. Despite my unintentional nap, I find myself to be quite exhausted.

It has rained recently enough that the ground still holds tracks quite clearly and so I set off, keeping a steady pace despite the jolts of pain every time I place a foot, bow in hand, Smith and Wesson tucked into my waistband, glad now that I decided to keep it despite my distaste towards guns. Other than the bullet used to slay the previous owner, it had a full clip, leaving me with 14 bullets. If the party I'm tracking are even half the size that they could be, I'm going to need all the help I can get.

\*

*The other guy stretches, luxuriously, in his warm nest of blankets, wriggling around and breathing deep the scent of the whore infused into the pillows and sheets that surround him. He potters around, wolfing down more dried meat, exploring her living area and storage areas to see what treasures she holds. His grudging respect for her grows as he sees how self sufficient and comparatively luxurious her life looks to be. The surviving remnants of humanity have effectively been reduced to the age of rocks and fire, suckling dry the remnants of technology from days past with no knowledge or ability to replicate it, and here she is with goddamned* electricity. *She has a water heater for fucks sake! She's probably the only person to have had a hot bath in North America in the last ten years. Not that the other guy wants a hot bath. He hasn't washed himself or his clothes in nearly a decade, beyond using cold water to remove dirt and dust when it caked up too much.*

*Her weapons cache though, that really caught his attention. Thousands of finely whittled, barbed darts and bottles of what he thought was belladonna, presumably to dip them in. Hundreds upon hundreds of arrows, beautifully balanced, wrapped in bark and straw and stacked in piles. Some with wickedly sharp flint heads, some merely a deadly sharp point. A few bows, handmade as far as he could see, but well made nonetheless. Another half a dozen machetes besides the one he pilfered, dozens of knives, made from metal or bone, of varying sizes. A well sealed bucket which on closer inspection seemed to contain clarified animal fat, lizard presumably, and there isn't all that much fat on a lizard so he felt it safe to assume that hundreds of lizard corpses had contributed to this one bucket. And next to it, a box with hundreds of...condoms? He barked out a humourless laugh, which surprised his own ears, and mulled over this discovery. He doubted she used them for their intended purpose, and so concluded, correctly, that she used the condoms to weaponise the fat.*

*This wasn't merely a defence cache. This woman, this* whore, *he reminded himself, was as much a hunter as her beast. He examines the harnesses and straps he comes across, and his cock twitches anew as he imagines pinioning her with her own gear before carrying out his violent fantasies. He examines pieces designed to armour the wearer and pieces designed to harness and hold various weapons and equipment. Something he sees sparks inspiration in his mind and he begins to hunt with purpose, seeking standalone straps that he can modify to his needs, collecting bandages along the way and scraps of leather.*

*He emerges from the cave with his stump wrapped and padded, first with bandages and then with leather, and crisscrossing up his arm are several leather straps, securely fastening the stolen machete to his arm. He has loaded a rucksack with dipped darts, wrapped carefully in cloth, an accompanying blowgun, food, painkillers, water tablets and the like, and deposited several of her fine knives around his person. Before he sets off his stomach rumbles again, and he spots a few snares set up in the tree-line and at least one captured lizard. He tests his new appendage first by cutting through the snare to release the lizard and then by chopping its head clean off. He is pleased with the results. An imperfect solution it may be, he knows this, but his left arm has a purpose again*

*He eats the lizard raw and relishes every cold, metallic, slippery bite.*

\*

*The beast laps prodigiously at the flowing river water, slaking a thirst that must be great, having sated a hunger that raged for hours and hours, through a whole night and the majority of the next day. Hours of dashing from tree to tree, bush to bush, snapping any lizard she saw in her jaws, crunching it down and immediately hunting for the next, moving aimlessly to all intents and purposes, following nose and instinct and nothing more. Her thirst quenched, she sits back on her haunches and gazes around her. Her tail twitches and swishes behind her, snagging on a small metal buckle which detaches and lands next to a front paw. She examines it, sniffs at it and in that moment also smells her own scent and that of two others, both familiar and yet unknown. She traces her own scent to clumps of fur snagged on adjacent thorn bushes but cannot find a source for the other two, beyond the metal buckle, which has the finest trace of both.*

*Working backwards from the river's edge, nose close to the ground, the two odours, now mixed with her own, split in several directions after a hundred meters or so. One trail, the trail that includes her own scent, leads to thick forestry and she knows all three scents come from this way, though she thinks at different times. A separate trail for each of the other two also splinter off in other directions, one leading back to the canyon, another heading up a small road, just visible past the treeline. The more she acquaints herself with the smell, the more aware she becomes of the guttural feelings deep in her chest. One, of loathing and rage, the other of...affection and warmth and loyalty.* Protectiveness.

*The beast chooses the complex trail with her own scent to follow first and pads along, into the trees, her sensitive nose following with no difficulty until she enters a clearing so thick with scent that she struggles at first to distinguish them from each other. When she is able to separate the various strains she follows one to the base of a tree to find her own brain matter splattered across the trunk. Her tail is rigid now, her ears perked but set slightly back, her fur raising across her hackles and shoulders as she finds the pile of vomit and semen, the dent in the earth next to it that smells warm and homely and the dent on the other side of the clearing that smells like white hot rage. And fear. The whole clearing reeks of fear.*

*She begins to remember now, stalking a man through the trees, leaping silently from branch to branch. The utter black of the night to her benefit, the anticipation growing in her chest as she draws closer and closer, the tang of his sweat and urine making her nose twitch even from a distance. The almost overwhelming joy that gripped her when she came to the edge of the trees, looking down on his greasy head, about to pounce and tear his head from his shoulders. Her paw slipping, just a touch, as she gathered herself and bunched her muscles ready to leap, and the tiniest crunch and creak that accompanied it. The man spinning, the sheen of terror balming his face. Blinding light. And then nothing.*

*She returns to the warm smell, the good smell and breathes deeply, immersing herself in it, willing for the connection, the memory to spark, and when the moment comes, it is less of a spark and more of a blazing inferno that consumes the beast and leaves in its place once again, the creature named Hope. With a blur of motion that is barely identifiable as anything at all, Hope is gone, in search of her Ayla, the setting sun seeming to set her fur alight in her wake.*

*

*The other guy follows the whore's tracks easily enough, the single line of her bike etched deeply into the still damp earth and dust. He had set off in the middle of the morning after devouring his raw treat and kept to a strong and steady pace through the day, only stopping to pass and collect water as needed. He chewed on dried meat as he jogged and marvelled at how well he felt already. He was not a man of science, the other guy, but he knew enough to know that he should still be bed bound and suffering from an injury like this, not bounding along on the trail of a whore like a teenager chasing his first whiff of pussy.*

*He did not understand his preternaturally swift recovery, but he also knew not to look proverbial gift recoveries in the mouth.*

*He came to the trailer where the one eyed bandit met his end as the light was lost and like the whore, thought it a suitable place to rest his head for the night. He didn't see that the large, dark spray on the ground was blood and brain matter, and he didn't venture behind the trailer to see the smorgasbord of appendages spread far and wide.*

*He did wake up though with a few more friends than when he went to sleep.*

# Chapter Fifteen

I wake with more aches and pains than I am happy with, knowing the challenges that lie ahead of me this day. The battered couch I slumbered on was comfortable enough but I slept poorly, twitching awake at every noise, real or imagined. The early morning sunlight streams through the window and I allow myself a few moments to centre myself. I followed the convoy's tracks for a few miles last night, stopping at a collection of houses and choosing the most dilapidated house in which to berth for the night, figuring it was the least likely to be looted in the event of bandits. I shot and roasted a lizard before settling to my uneasy slumber and I force myself to eat the remains, knowing I will need my energy, but the adrenaline looping through me every few seconds has destroyed my appetite and it feels akin to choking down strips of leather.

I'm uncharacteristically nervous and I take a few deep breaths to try and slow my heart and still my nerves. My chest feels odd, almost full and for a few moments I struggle to even take a full breath. This is not my preferred setting for a hunt. I know nothing about my opponents, not even the size of their party, but given the paucity of my supplies and my limited opportunity to recover my bike, I feel truly that I have little choice.

I drain the water I have left and refill my canteen from the cistern in the back of this house, dropping in half a tablet to purify, and re hook it to my belt. I step outside the house and *listen,* stilling myself entirely to pick up on any available noise, tuning out the sound of my own heartbeat and holding my breath. I hear the faintest sound of engines, multiple, coming from the direction of the tracks I've been following. They're already on the move. I had hoped to start before them and make some ground. I'll have to run at maximum capacity to have a hope of catching them today, and that relies on their passage being slowed by obstacles on the road. A shiver of unease rolls through me as I consider the possibility that I might not catch them. I *need* that bike back. Hopefully they'll make more stops than I will. They have no reason to think that I, or anyone, could catch them on foot after all. I set off, heading north east, tracking my prey with fear in my heart for the first time in many years.

*

My toe catches on a rock mid run and my usually sharp reflexes fail me, sending me tumbling to the ground with all the grace of a wounded sow. I lie in the dust, winded, trying to draw breath, and curse my inattention. Several hours of running without a break has taken its toll, both on my physical and mental stamina, but I know I've gained some ground. I am close enough now to catch the occasional shout on the wind and laid on the ground as I am, can easily hear the rumble of tires with my ear pressed to the earth. They are only a few miles ahead but until they stop moving, I'm unlikely to catch them. I may have to come upon them when they stop for the night.

I turn onto my back, air now filling my lungs freely, and take a few minutes to rest, swigging small sips from my water. My ears seem to be buzzing, and I shake my head to try and clear it, without success. I focus on the sound, which seems to be coming from my own head rather than an external source. Buzzing is the wrong word…it's more of a...pulsing? Not quite sound but not quite sensation. Each little...pulse, sends a small wave of fear through me, and once again I know the fear is not my own, despite having my share of anxiety about the meeting to come. The sensation is so faint that had I not stopped running, I might never have noticed it, but now that I am still, it can't be ignored.

The pulsing feels familiar and in that moment I know that it is the hidden figure from the hospital, communicating terror far and wide. I close my eyes, almost in defeat, knowing that my task is now all the more difficult, for how can I ignore a cry for help that has landed directly in my own head? Planning an attack with the survival of others in mind is so much more difficult than planning an attack whose purpose is pure annihilation. Their terror must be great indeed to be reaching me from this far away, and at that thought I receive a pulse that is more of a bolt, and almost painful in its intensity. I find myself gripped by that same terror, mouth dry, pulse racing and echoing in my ears, palms instantly slick and will myself to breathe, slowly, trying to slow my thumping heart and regain control of my own senses. I cannot allow myself to be consumed by their terror, not when I have my own fear to contend with.

I focus on the pulsing and imagine myself raising a barrier, no...a filter. I want to feel the pulse but not the terror, as I can see the benefit to this connection if fostered. At first it feels impossible, like trying to manipulate a water balloon generously coated in petroleum jelly. As soon as I get a grip it slips and slides, and seems to snap back to the metaphorical start but after a few attempts I learnt to dig in with ghostly fingers and wrestle it back into place, until the channel to my mind is coated with a slick, transparent layer. I can still sense the terror but it no longer floods my own feelings, leaving me alone with my own emotions again. I am disconcerted to discover that my own fear is now heightened and my heart raps and thuds in my ears all by itself.

My chest still feels curiously full, though the sensation no longer prevents me from drawing a full breath. It reminds me of the feeling of being connected to Hope, and I am dismayed at the tears that spring almost instantly to my eyes at the thought of her. Grief is a funny thing. You can almost forget about it in times of distraction, but the sensation can wallop you over the head and consume your being at the slightest provocation. I recall the first few weeks after losing Tilly to be much the same, a constant ebb of sorrow interspersed with painful lances of pure agony, only not felt when consumed by another action, and I had little to distract me for those first few terrifying months. At least the days following Hope's demise have provided ample distraction from the crushing grief I felt upon realising, finally that she was lost to me.

I wonder at this new connection. It feels similar to the conduit I shared with Hope, more powerful if anything, and I compare it to what I felt upon meeting the young woman who pointed her gun at my head. I was able to get a sense of her general demeanour and emotions, but had no sense that the connection travelled the other way. Had that been the case, the woman would have known that my intentions to her and the unseen figure were not malicious. It was clear though from the interaction, that the woman was at least receiving the same signals as I.

Is there something different about me, that allows me to both receive and return these pulses, or signals, or whatever they are? I had assumed that my curious link with Hope was entirely down to her unique nature, but this new discovery, as well as the significant physical changes wrought in me, clearly not mirrored in the woman from the hospital, make me question this. Despite my recent bruising, my skin is relatively unmarked now, my old scars seeming to have disappeared. The dust no longer seems able to adhere to me and my eyes of course have changed radically. The woman, though beautiful, had skin clearly marked by scars, and her eyes were a dark pool without a hint of my new, bright gold. She had the bubbled scar tissue that I have yet to see another human without.

I linger over this thought as I push to my feet and renew my punishing pace. I've seen the corpses of many men, and some women and children since civilisation collapsed, and I've yet to see a body without the creeping scars. I make a point of checking. While the Bubble Flu consumed my family and our animals within the space of a single day, I never even had a tickle in my throat. I had always assumed that I was simply one of the lucky immune few, but what if rather than having an immunity, my body was able to adapt the virus? Perhaps those mammals gestated during or after the plague are born with this adaptation in place? If only there were some semblance of resources remaining to us that would allow a thorough exploration of this phenomenon. I have no illusions where this is concerned. I've yet to even encounter a group or individual who uses batteries for electricity as I do, let alone any more advanced technology. The plague killed without discrimination, and the massacres of those remaining heavily favoured the brutish and violent. Perhaps there is no brain remaining in the world capable of formulating an answer to this question, and even if there is, with what could they answer it?

The light is warmer now and the sky is streaked with red, marking the demise of another day. Hopefully the party I track will soon stop for the night, and I fervently hope that they do so in a position which will allow me some measure of tactical advantage. The land through which we travel though is largely flat and open, a few rolling hills and dilapidated buildings, very little in the way of tree cover, so I fear my hope is for nothing. There are a multitude of trees in the park in which I live, fed by the great river and its offspring, which formed part of my basis for choosing it, but outside of this once protected and cultivated region, the land surrounding me is fairly barren.

The further I run, the more urgent the pulsing in my head becomes. I am able still to filter out the fear, but that doesn't reduce my awareness of it and when I become aware of the engines cutting out and the heightened noises of rambunctious men calling to each other as they set up their camp, that fear spikes to a crescendo that almost drives me to my knees. The ease with which the sound carries to me tells me that the ground between us lies open and flat, and indeed I cannot see anything that would suggest otherwise on the horizon. It is almost full dark now, and I estimate I am still several miles away, at least five, possibly more. Despite my stamina and fitness, I am beginning to fail, and my strong pace has been reduced to just above a jog.

I stop and allow myself fifteen minutes of rest, sipping my water and eating the last leg of last night's lizard. All the while the pulsing has now become a pounding against the inside of my skull and on more than one occasion the pounding is accompanied by a single word. *Help.* I don't know if the hidden figure knows I'm out here, following, or if they are simply broadcasting their terror far and wide without realising, but I instinctively know that my own reach does not extend far enough to send a message in return.

Whatever this unknown creature is, it is more powerful than I, at least where this ability is concerned.

# Chapter Sixteen

A few miles later, I crest a small hill and stop, dropping to the ground and laying on my front, as the party I track comes into my sight for the first time. Dropping to the ground might have been unnecessary; they are still at least two miles ahead of me, and only the open flat expanse and my own preternaturally good eyesight has allowed me to see them from so far. Their giant bonfire helps, illuminating the surrounding land for several hundred yards in every direction. This is a group with no fear of attack, and I am swiftly able to see why. I continue to approach the group, maintaining my pace until I start coming to the outer reaches of the ring of light surrounding them, when I slow and begin duckwalking and observing.

I count eighteen men, seated or standing around the fire, and observe from the scattered bones that they have already ingested their evening meal. At least five of the men have guns at their hips and all are equipped with large knives, machetes or hammers. The vehicles are clustered on my side of the camp, and I ease behind the cover of a large truck with the label Ford just above the bumper to more securely continue my observations. There are two men casually ambling around the perimeter, but it's clear from their lingering glances that they are more concerned with the scene being played out in the centre of the group than their surroundings. One passes a few meters in front of me without noticing my presence.

The men all roughly face the same direction, focusing on the kneeling woman and the man that looms over her, a giant brute by anyone's standards. The woman is, as suspected, the woman from the hospital, and my stomach flips when I take in her state of undress and her demeanour, head bowed, shoulders shaking, whole body seeming to tremble. The man towers above the others in the group, none of whom look particularly small. His face is pitted and pocked with scars and his right eye is just a crater, scored with an angry red line, left by whichever weapon claimed his eye. He looks down at the woman with amused contempt, stroking the length of the bullwhip clutched in his fist, slowly and deliberately. Light glints off the knuckles of his left hand and I see that he wears chunky knuckledusters.

The woman's back is to me but I'm clearly able to see the fresh welts crisscrossing her back, buttocks and shoulders and the dappled bruising well, everywhere. The lack of fresh blood leads me to think those are last night's injuries. I continue scanning the group, trying to find the hidden figure from before. It is definitely here; the pulsing tells me that and since becoming aware of it, I wouldn't have even needed the tracks to continue following the group, had they become too eroded to follow. The pulsing would have led me to them like a beacon.

A metallic clatter catches my attention, and I direct my gaze to the far side of the camp where I see, locked in a cage that was probably once designed for a dog, a child. A human child, who is gazing directly into my eyes. *Help, help, please help, please help, please help,* **please help, please help us!** The words beat against my skull like a drumbeat and I will her to stop and quiet so I can concentrate on what is to come.

I lock eyes with her and simply think, *Okay, I'll try,* and the battering calms and fades, until I am alone in my head again. The child is seated with her knees drawn up to her chest, a collar securely fastened around her neck and attached to the cage and I observe that when not looking into her eyes, she is curiously difficult to focus on, as though my eyes want to slip through her or past her. Which explains why I didn't immediately spot her when making my initial observations. Her skin seems to have the same shimmering quality that mine now exhibits, but accentuated, and those eyes are the same pure gold as my darling Hope. With that thought another spike of grief lances through me, and the child examines me with curiosity, having clearly shared the emotion but perhaps not the meaning behind it. I feel the probing of ghostly fingers in my head again and instinctively throw up a firmer barrier.

*Now is not the time!*

The child dips her head in seeming consternation and I focus my gaze again on the main party. She seems safe for now and now I know her location, I can endeavour to avoid throwing any projectiles her way. I allow myself a moment to wish for my fat filled balloons; the position of the giant brute would have allowed me to spray him with my homemade napalm quite effectively, but my little paint tin and balloons are nestled in my saddlebags on my bike...which in my distraction, I failed to notice is in fact laid on the flatbed of the very truck against which I currently lean. I duckwalk along to the back of the truck and peer over the lip. I can just reach the clip on one of the bags. I don't want to risk the noise of clambering into the truck, or pulling the bike closer to me, but if I open it from here, any contents will clatter straight out onto the truck bed.

I pull back in frustration as the deepest voice I've ever heard reaches my ears. I can almost *feel* it more than I can hear it.

"Such a silly little whore to think you could escape our reach. Such an *ungrateful* little whore to run in the first place. Did we not feed you and the child? Did we not protect you from the uncivilised that roam these lands? Years we kept you and that demon child safe from harm, years when other, lesser men would have eaten you at the first suggestion of hunger. What manner of repayment is this?"

I hear no answer words from the woman kneeling at his feet, and expect to hear none. The questions are clearly rhetorical.

"Are you sorry yet?"

I hear a murmur from the woman, followed by meaty crack as the giant slaps her with an open hand. Unfortunately this is the hand that wears the dusters, and the poor woman goes down like a sack of rocks. I creep back around the truck in time to see him twist a fist in her hair, lift her and drop her back on her knees, where she sways but manages to stay upright.

He repeats the question and again the woman murmurs a response, but her voice is curiously muffled, as though speaking through a wad of fabric. This time he whips her across the face and as she falls onto her back, I see the ruin of her mouth and understand why she can't speak the words he is asking her for. Her mouth and jaw are grotesquely swollen and as she opens her mouth wide, gasping for air, my enhanced vision allows me to see that her teeth and tongue are both gone. My heart rate quickens at the inherent sadism of this. This isn't punishment, this is torture.

The giant drops her back onto her knees again and squats before her, smiling gently and stroking her cheek, lifting her chin so he was looking directly into her eyes as he spoke again.

"Speak the words or we'll all fuck your daughter like we fucked you last night, and then we'll see how sorry you really are."

The woman starts babbling hysterically, the words mushy and unformed as they spill from her mouth, her meaning clear even if her words were not. The giant laughs and stands, whipping her again across her tortured mouth and she curls into a ball, sobbing into her hands and the dirt. I can feel the terror and the helplessness rolling off her in waves and I want to intervene now, but I still haven't the semblance of a plan to take on this many men, and know I must resist until an opportune moment presents itself.

The giant takes a few, slow, deliberate steps towards the cage, looking over his shoulder to watch the woman's reaction and she pushes to her knees, scrabbling after him, reaching out to grasp at his hems, nonsensical sound pouring from her mouth. He kicks her onto her back and kicks her, hard, in the groin, stopping her in her tracks. He surveys her prone form, the smile never leaving his face and squats beside her again.

"There is something else you can do, to prove how sorry you are."

The woman looks up at him through floods of tears, nodding fervently, strings of drool mixing with the water pouring from her eyes and dripping off her jaw and chin. He pulls a small switchblade from his belt and flicks it open, admiring the light rolling over the blade before holding the knife out to the prone woman, who stared at it in surprise, clearly afraid to take it from him.

"If we're going to keep you again, I need some assurance that you won't try any more funny business. No more running, no late night sneak attacks."

The woman nods, desperately.

"But I can't take your word this time, since you promised me that before. I'm going to need something more concrete." The giant snaps his fingers and one of the watching men approaches him and drops the machete he's holding next to the giant. The woman stares at the machete and the knife, and then back to the giant, clearly none the wiser as to his intentions, though I have a sick feeling growing in my stomach as I begin to piece together what he will ask of her.

"Cut off your foot and cut out your eye, and we'll hold off on using the kid as a fuckpuppet at least until she gets her bleeders."

The woman's eyes widen as his request sinks in. The child begins pounding at my brain again, her panic rising as she realises what is about to happen. I try to keep her out because I need to *think* and I need to make my move if I have any hope of preventing this. I see now the folly in trying to use the fat as a weapon, since an attack with that will just as likely kill the woman as any of the men. I take a deep breath. Darts, then arrows, then gun then hand to hand? I might be able to avoid them locating me until I switch to the gun if I keep moving, and I need to take down the men with guns as a priority, as much as I want to send an arrow through the giants remaining eye right now.

I unstrap my bow and loosen the fastenings on my knives, axe and machete, before checking the fastenings on the gloves and kneepads. I don't have my helmet or boot mods, more's the pity. They're both in my saddlebags and I can't risk the noise of trying to obtain them. Without my boot mods however my passage is almost silent, which will give me a small advantage at least to start.

As I palm the dart gun and load a dart, blowing it at the side of the neck nearest to me and immediately moving a few meters to my left, loading another, the men all clap their hands to their ears in unison. A few drop to their knees, the agony evident on their faces.

I glance at the child and see her mouth wide open in a silent scream, tendons in her neck standing out in relief and surmise that she must be sending out some sort of mental shriek that is incapacitating the men. I take a moment to be grateful that she is able to filter who she targets and see the giant leave the woman's side, stumbling across to the cage, clearly intent on stopping the child's mental onslaught.

I blow that dart, scoring another neck hit on the giant and circle to my left again, loading as I go. The giant reaches the child's cage and she closes her mouth and shrinks back in fear, and I blow another dart in his direction, hoping to distract his attention before he crushes her skull in his hands, his intention clear as day. I hit below his right ear and yes, he's turning back in my direction as I continue my circle of the camp. I score three more direct hits before the group have recovered from the psychic attack and are turning and actively searching for the source of the darts. By this time I've circled to the other side of the group and am a dozen meters or so behind the giant, still low enough that in the contrast of black night and blazing fire, I am not immediately visible to the group, who are facing the wrong way, barking orders to each other and spreading in a different directions, intent on finding their mystery attacker.

They are clearly disoriented by the girl's apparently brutal attack and my unexpected ambush, but these men are seasoned killers and I know it won't take them long to recover. I grasp my bow and nock an arrow, aiming for one of the men with a gun at his hip, shooting him clean through the back of the neck. He drops like a stone and I bolt to my left again, sprinting a dozen meters until I have the cover of the cars once more. Nocking another arrow I shoot for the first man to lay eyes on me, spearing him straight through his open mouth before he can articulate his shout and give me away. I shoot the next man through the eye and swiftly reload my bow, too swiftly, for I fumble the next shot and take the next man in the shoulder. The right shoulder thankfully, since he was reaching for his gun. His arm is instantly useless but he has seen me and has directed the attention of the thirteen other remaining men towards me.

The surprise in their faces at seeing their attacker is but a woman is almost comical, and I take advantage of their momentary distraction, finishing off the guy I shot in the shoulder with another arrow to the eye and swiftly launching another to the throat of the man next to him, who by chance rather than design was another of the men with a gun. Three gunmen down, two others down, thirteen to go. The men are running for me now and I bolt, keeping to my left and fire wildly over my shoulder. I hear a squelch as it connects, like a stone dropped into mud from a height, and the corresponding thud of his body hitting the ground, but can't stop to confirm the kill, I have to keep running. Twelve to go, hopefully, but I feel panic beginning to creep into my stomach, because twelve is *too many* to be taking on now that my cover is blown. I try to pick up the pace and fire another arrow behind me but in that split second of glancing behind me I trip over something metallic with a clatter and hit the ground with all of the force of my sprint behind me.

I roll back onto my feet but I've lost my grip on the bow, my hands are now empty and they've gained almost all the ground I had on them. Grasping fingers brush my right shoulder and I force myself to run *faster, faster* and manage to pull ahead by a few feet. I *push* out with my mind, willing the child to help again and am rewarded by agonised bellows behind me, coupled with several thuds as several of the men fall to their knees. By this time I have run back around to the cars again and I risk a glance over my shoulder, to see six of the men huddled on the ground, hands over their ears, and the others stumbling aimlessly, faces screwed up in agony.

All except the giant, who seems less affected than the others. I lock eyes with him and that's when I see what I missed before, the gun he pulls from the back of his waistband and understand that the bullet is not for me but for the child. He gives me that smile, that *shit eating grin* and turns from me, with no fear of turning his back, since have I not dropped my bow? The child's fear upon seeing the gun turn in her direction is so acute that it bleeds through my filter and her mental scream stops in its tracks.

I reach for my gun in desperation and squeeze off a shot before I've even aimed at the giant, hoping to at least distract him before he pulls his trigger, and am rewarded with a start as he turns back in my direction. I squeeze the trigger again as another man collides with me from the side, taking me to the ground in a vicious tackle. My bullet connects with the giant's leg and he drops to the ground as I fire another at my attacker, blowing his skull apart and showering myself in blood and brain matter. I push him off me, no easy feat with that dead weight, and roll just as a machete is buried in the ground where my head lay only a split second before. I yelp in spite of myself and keep rolling, pivoting onto my feet and shoot the machete wielder in the face, blasting him backwards off his feet to collide with the man behind him, taking them both to the ground. Another swift bullet to the man pinned to the ground and I have nine opponents left.

I bring the gun to shoulder height and pick off another three in a row, headshots all, and some distant part of my brain marvels at the accuracy of those shots, all the while reminding myself that there is no victory until victory is complete. If my count is correct I have six bullets left and six men to kill. Perhaps this won't be so hard after all. I shoot the guy closest to the child's cage, who I spotted with his gun in his hand, and just have time to observe that I can only see four men, not five, when a crashing blow thunders into my right temple, hitting the same spot as did the one eyed bandit so recently. My legs turn into jelly beneath me and I go down seeing stars, curling instinctively into a ball as the men, excepting the giant, surround me and begin landing vicious kicks to my back, ribs and legs.

I feel something crack in my chest and know at least one of my ribs is gone already, pain piercing my side every time I draw a breath, and know I have seconds, if that, to make a move before one of those kicks shatters my spine and I am permanently incapacitated. The gun is still clutched in my right hand and I sneak the barrel through the gap between my left arm and left leg, pulling the trigger blindly. I'm rewarded with an impact, a deafening blast of sound, and the instant loss of the hearing in my left ear, but the men fall back and the kicks are halted. I spring to my feet and shoot the guy directly in front of me with the pistol, splitting his mouth open and spraying teeth across the ground but almost immediately lose my balance, dropping back to my knees, the concussive effects of the blow to my head and the pistol discharging so close to me destroying my equilibrium. I grapple to regain my feet but my world is spinning and I can't tell which way is up anymore. The ground rises to meet my face and I can't even get my arms out in time, taking the full force of the landing on my chin, and I feel the telltale warm trickle of blood evacuating my body.

Rough hands grab me by the ankle and drag me back towards the bonfire, face down. I blearily focus on the trail of blood that I leave in my wake and am surprised even in my concussed state at how much I am bleeding. I manage to roll onto my back and plant a boot in the backside of the guy dragging me along, propelling him, to my satisfaction, straight into the bonfire, which is now only a few meters in front of me. The heat is searing even from this distance and I have a moment of pity for the man, who didn't even get out a dying scream before the flames robbed him of his ability to do so.

The moment is over quickly as the remaining lackey stomps hard on my right hand, still clutching the gun in a death grip, and I hear several cracks and pops as my fingers are shattered. He leans down to pick up the gun, rather than kicking it away, and this is his undoing as he is one of the five I struck with my darts. His balance fails him and as he topples over I unsheathe my beloved bowie and bury it in the back of his neck with my good left hand.

His body drops onto my legs, the phrase deadweight an apt one, as for the life of me I can't shift him off with only the use of one hand to help. I hear the dragging shuffle of the giant as he strides up to me, clearly favouring his wounded leg, and he picks up the dead guy effortlessly in one of his shovel-like hands, tossing him to the side as though discarding a piece of paper. The corpse lands in the bonfire beside his comrade, sending up a cascade of sparks and embers which settle on the giant, but he pays them no more mind than I might pay a small insect buzzing in my vicinity.

That same shovel of a hand grips my neck and drags me to my feet, before slamming my whole body back to the floor again, cracking another rib and forcing all of the air out of my lungs. I gasp, desperate to pull some air into my lungs and finding myself entirely unable to before I am lifted into the air and hurled to the ground again, fury contorting his face into a mask even more grotesque than his own, unlovely features. After a third slam which seems to paralyse me entirely, he straddles my hips and locks his hands around my throat.

My vision instantly dims and while I can just about feel my arms again, his reach is so great that my hands can barely connect past his elbows. I can only bat at him ineffectively as the darkness begins to swallow me and within seconds I see nothing, hear nothing more than the rushing in my ears, and feel only the fire in my lungs as they struggle to expand to no avail.

From the darkness behind my eyes a face blooms, the face of my lovely Tilly, my mother's behind her, young and beautiful, unmarked by the passage of time and the battering of fists. A face I only knew from faded photographs, brought to sharp, clear life before me. They smile with their eyes and reach for me with their hands and I know that I am done, I am ready, I am willing and able to go with them. My fingers brush Tilly's and my heart cracks open, spilling forth all the love and grief that had been contained within since I lost her and her sweet, sweet voice reaches my ears, singing the song I sang to her as she died, her voice pure and true where mine was cracked and hoarse and torn with pain.

*Sleep and rest where you are safe,*
*My darling dear rest your eyes,*
*There's a place in my embrace,*
*Where nightmares flee and no one dies.*

*I'll circle you within my arms,*
*And surround you with only my love,*
*No pain, no fear, only still calm,*
*I'll shield you with my love, my love.*

"You can rest now, Mother. You did your best, for all of us. We love you."

I stare at my little girl, who looks back at me with impossible wisdom in her eyes, those beautiful blue eyes, so similar to my own, shining with tears like celestial bodies, and I swear in that moment I can see every star in the heavens reflected in her eyes. I try to grasp her hand but cannot, her fingers slip through mine like sand and instead of coming closer and clearer, the image of her and Mother begins to fade, fade, fade away, slipping into greyness and then into black and I think to myself, *finally, this is it.*

But instead of increasing, the darkness lifts a little and the pressure around my throat eases, as a scaldingly hot liquid sprays in copious volume across my face. The blackness lifts in time for me to see the expression of surprised horror on the giant's face as the switchblade completes its journey across his throat, splitting him from ear to ear in a bloody grin far more satisfying than the smirk on his face only minutes earlier. I push him to the side with my left arm, gasping desperately for air through my wheezing throat, and see another pair of hands doing the same, while I pivot my hips to give him the momentum to roll onto his side rather than planting straight down onto me. Given his bulk, I'm not sure that that wouldn't kill me all by itself.

I remain on my back, shaking and shivering, wheezing and spluttering, tears streaming over my bloody cheeks and chin from the sight and sound of those I have lost. Did they truly come to help me pass over or was it just a trick of my traumatised and dying mind? Does Tilly know that I am her mother? Do they still exist, out there somewhere, waiting for me to come to them at last?

I focus on my saviour, the young woman kneeling beside me, switchblade still clutched in her hand, the other hand holding my good one. Even through the ruin of her face I can see the gratitude shining from her eyes and in the tears that also flood her face. I try to tell her it's ok, it's over now, she and her daughter are safe, but when I open my mouth no sound comes out, excepting a tortured wheeze, and she shakes her head, moving to stroke my face. I catch her hand, quickly, for she still grasps the knife with a death grip, and massage her knuckles until she opens her fist and drops the blade. She touches my face, oh so gently, fingertips tracing from my bloody chin to my battered temple.

I hold her other hand in my good one, pulling it to my chest and rest, just for a moment, afraid to close my eyes in case I don't open them again, and more afraid that a big part of me *wants* that. All of these years and my fight, my *need* for survival has always been so strong, but a few moments ago it bled out of me entirely. I was so ready. *So tired* of fighting for every breath in this hideous fucking world. So tired of the pain, and the loss, and the grief. Mother, Tilly, Hope. Cruelty is king here, and what can one woman do to fight against it? My eyes slip closed, I focus on the rhythm of those gentle fingers and feel pressure against my left hand, know that the woman desperately wants me to stay present, stay awake, stay with her and the child, but all I want to do now is sleep. The fear has passed and I would sleep forever if I could.

Until a stinging sensation to the side of my neck brings me crashing back into my body. My eyes fly open and I shake off her hand, reaching for my neck, my fingers grasping at the dart embedded in me, one of *my* darts. I meet her eyes, those deep, liquid, *beautiful* eyes and catch the expression of horror in them before they are rent apart from pressure within, pushed out in opposite directions and the life in them instantly departs, rendered dull and glassy. I try to shout, to scream, to say *anything* but my voice breaks apart and all that comes out is a strangled croak. Her corpse is shoved to one side and rising from behind her, staring down at me with pure, unbridled contempt in his eyes, is the other guy.

# Chapter Seventeen

He stands over me, *the other guy*, my fucking nemesis it would seem. I note with vague interest that his left arm is missing, well half of it, and he seems to have attached a machete to the stump, *my favourite fucking machete* at that. The blood and gore dripping from the blade to congeal on the ground tell me that this was the weapon that finished the once beautiful young woman, and I know that even if I manage to wrest it from his grasp, or lack thereof, I will never use that blade again. His unusual silhouette strikes me as oddly funny and I find myself barking out a hacking laugh, a response so inappropriate to the situation that it brings me immediately to my senses and I realise that I am as high as the proverbial fucking kite.

The child's mental scream of anguish and grief pierces my throbbing skull and I arch my back and grit my teeth, letting out a hoarse shriek of my own. Either my defences are down or her pain is too great to be contained, as I cannot block out the banshee cry, nor can I filter out her towering, shattering agony as she realises her mother is slain. I hear heavy footsteps heading towards the child and her cage and the shimmering ring of rending metal as he opens the cage and drags her from inside. I manage to open my eyes a slit and see her passage stopped as suddenly as it started as the collar and lead around her neck snap taught, and the pain stops as suddenly as it came. I hope that he will just leave her now and start dragging myself in their direction, hoping to distract him, but he uses his machete arm to slice through the lead and pull her from the cage. He tosses her to the ground and delivers one, sickeningly hard kick to her head, and just like that, I cannot feel her anymore.

I try to lift myself to my knees, to my feet, but my right hand is useless and my legs are made of elastic, snapping me back to the ground as soon as I get a knee or a foot under me. I hear his footsteps to my left and feel his fist twist in my hair as he drags me backwards. I try to grab his hand, twist, pivot, even to kick out behind me but I fail to make contact and every shift off the ground makes the ground roll as though we are on water, not packed dirt and earth. I lean to the side and vomit, suddenly, evacuating what little remained in my stomach but he does not pause or break, simply keeps dragging me until we reach a low metal chair.

He tosses me on my back and I see the rucksack next to the chair, which he digs into, clearly discounting me as an opponent now, and with fair reason since at this point I can't even hold myself upright, try as I might. I feel a familiar weight at my hip and remember that incapacitated as I am, I am still armed, and while he pulls out leather straps and knives from the rucksack, I very slowly and carefully remove the axe from my belt. I wait for him to turn and face me again as I cannot reach any part other than his legs from my angle, and as he turns back to me I swing the axe, aiming for his jaw or neck, knowing this is my last chance, my last hurrah, and on the wind I could swear I hear the strains of singing reaching my ears.

He twists and lowers his chin at the last moment, so my axe is buried in the meat of his shoulder rather than his neck, and he howls at me in pain and fury, his face distorted beyond recognition. He tears the axe from his shoulder, spraying me with yet more blood and straddles me like the giant, but instead of strangling me he rains blow after blow into my unprotected face, punctuating each blow with an exclamation of rage.

"You fucking *whore,* it's time to learn your *lesson,* you'll fucking learn from *this, you goddamned fucking whore!"*

The weight lifts from my hips and I know some real damage has been done. My nose feels shattered, there's at least one new gap in the teeth of my lower jaw and when I try to open my eyes, I find them swollen almost shut, and the little vision between the lids is blurry. Something hot leaks from my right ear and when I pull my fingers away, I see vivid blood.

I am lifted bodily and thrown down across the low chair, reawakening the fire in my ribs, but I feel curiously far away, almost as though my body isn't mine anymore. I can feel all of my injuries but it's as though I can't feel the pain anymore. He lashes my wrists behind me, grinding the bones of my shattered hand together and pinions my ankles, before sawing through my belt and pulling my trousers down to my knees. He lets out a guffaw at whatever it is he sees and I wonder what could possibly be funny about the sight of my vagina.

"You've got your bleeders you filthy bitch! Lucky for you I suppose, I wasn't planning on using anything to lube you up. I wanted you to feel every inch of my cock tearing you apart!"

I must be miscarrying. I don't share this with the other guy. I suspect it would increase his ardour even more.

*

*He gazes at her bloody genitals, the redness exciting him beyond belief and savours this moment, that has consumed him for these many days past, since he first had the whore pinioned and at his mercy. He wasn't able to finish the job then, but nothing will interrupt him now. He pulls out his cock and starts stroking it, building his erection, preparing for the sweet moment of entry he has been dreaming about, dragging his head across her lips, feeling the shudder that rolls through her at the sensation. He recalls the glorious moment from before when she gagged at the sensation of him entering her, and he can no longer resist, lining himself up with her entrance and readying himself to push inside.*

*At that moment he also recalls the growl that vibrated in his bones, the terror of his mutilation at the jaws of the beast, and the consequences of his last attack on the whore, and he finds he is instantly flaccid and incapable of gaining entry. His pulse pounds in his ears, his palms are slick and his mouth is dry as he grips his cock in hand again, stroking himself, trying to build his lust, but every time he looks down at her filthy cunt he remembers the terror anew, until he is gasping for breath and sweating profusely.*

*The whore's shoulders are shaking, presumably with fear…or…wait.*

*Is she laughing? She's fucking laughing at him? He who now holds all the power in the world over her? She must be out of her fucking mind!*

\*

I can't contain my mirth any longer and I'm rasping and coughing, almost giggling to myself at the mental image I have of the other guy, flaccid dick in hand, trying desperately to maintain his erection so he can give me the revenge raping of his dreams. He had no issue on our last encounter, so presumably this is a new problem for him. I know my laughter is reckless but I'm not naive; I'm dead no matter what I do. I can at least have some fun in my passing.

"What's the matter big boy? Not enough man juice to prop up your pathetic worm today?"

He all but *screams* in rage. If he was unhinged before, he's off the map now. He leans down to my ear.

"If I can't fuck you with cock, I'll find a suitable substitute. I spotted a few guns lying around. How about one of those? Then I can shoot you through your disgusting whore *cunt,* and while you slowly bleed to death from the inside I'll cut you up piece by piece and eat you while you're still alive!"

Yup. Deranged. My body feels further and further away and my chest is filling with emotions, all wrong to my situation. Hope and warmth and yes, anger, but also power and freedom. Maybe this is just my brain protecting me again, knowing that I am about to pass, for the second time today.

His footsteps retreat and then return and he dangles his hand before my eyes, the long barrel of a handgun I don't recognise clutched in his fist.

"Will that do, *whore?* It's not as thick as my cock but it's nice and long and you should feel every cold inch right up to your fucking *womb.*"

I close my eyes as I feel the cold metal press against me. I feel further and further removed from my body, drifting almost aimlessly away. It's not a great way to go but hell, it's not like I ever had a long life expectancy. As a deep, deep calm descends upon me, I hear Hope's growl rolling through my mind, and wish that she was here as before, wish I could feel that rumble deep in my chest as before, and like magic I do, filling my lungs and seeming to tickle my heart. Oh the tricks my brain will pull to give me comfort in my passing! I focus on that growling, the hope, yes the HOPE that it gives me, and realise that the other guy has withdrawn the gun, *because he can hear it too*! My heart leaps into my throat and I cry out, in joy, in hope and in *fucking pain* because it seems as though I have reconnected with every part of my body at once and I can feel *everything*.

There is fire in my chest, rage and biting metallic fury, and I know this is Hope I feel again, my Hope who has somehow, *somehow* returned for me. The growl rolls across the ground again, vibrating in my very bones and tears pour  anew from my eyes, tears of pure, sheer, unadulterated joy and with a rending, glutinous tear that sounds like the sweetest music ever conceived, the other guy finally leaves this world.

# Chapter Eighteen

I struggle for several minutes, even with Hope's sure, solid presence at my back, to bring my arms in front of me, as mirrored by the events that led us here in the first place and struggle for several minutes more to saw through the sturdy leather straps holding me, even with my own, finely honed blades. I am displeased to see that these bindings also belong to me, and conclude that the other guy must have returned to my dwelling once I left to raid my stores. My dominant hand, the right, is completely useless and Hope, multi skilled as she is, lacks the opposable thumbs necessary to help me with this. So she remains at my back, supporting me as I saw painstakingly through the straps, first at my wrists and then at my ankles. I turn and take in my lovely girl, blood dripping from the corners of her mouth as she bares her teeth at me in what is unmistakably a grin, and throw my arms around her great shoulders, uncontrollable sobs wracking my body as it sinks in that she's here, she's *alive,* I'm not *alone anymore.*

We remain like this for some time, until my sobs have reduced to hiccups and sniffles, Hope sitting patiently as my tears and blood soak into her fur, such beautiful fur, and my heart could burst from the pure force of the varying emotions that threaten to overwhelm me. Joy so extreme that I feel there must be a more apt word available to me, towering grief at the loss of the woman and child, sheer relief that the fight is done and that Hope's presence will protect me for now. Emotions are radiating from Hope as well; satisfaction, traces of lingering anger, relief, joy of her own and *love.*

As the child crosses my mind again, Hope shifts her weight as though she wants to get up. I pull my arms back, cradling my right hand as she limberly rises to her feet and pads over to the little corpse a few meters away from us. She sniffs at her as I manage to push to my knees and then my feet, pleased that my equilibrium is returning, though I can still see the effects of the drugged dart in the patterns of the flames rising from the bonfire, now beginning to burn low, casting red light over the entire scene. The effect is eerie and I shudder in spite of myself, as I take in the corpses littering the ground, the blood spattered far and wide, the pieces of people that should rightfully be inside them, separated from their bodies.

Hope whines to get my attention and I turn my gaze to her, and the child, wondering what she could possibly want me to do. It is clear from the angle of her neck and *holy fucking shitfire,* the dent in her skull, that the child is beyond help, and I turn away from the sight, not wanting to witness any more death this night. Hope gives a little bark this time and trots over to me, gripping my arm gently in her jaws and pulling me over to the child. She nudges the back of my knee with her head and sighing in resignation, I kneel beside her, trying not to look at the dent, or the unnatural angle too closely. I feel for a pulse, knowing this is hopeless because even if by some miracle she is still alive, surely she will be brain de-

She has a pulse. It is faint and fluttering beneath my fingers, but that is definitely a pulse. I look over my shoulder at Hope. She whines at me again, softly, and I recall the catastrophic injury that Hope must have sustained and recovered from, the swift healing of my own injuries, the absurd recovery of the other guy from having his arm half torn off and then amputated. This child seems to be more special than any of us, from what I've seen so far. Maybe she has a chance to beat this. I owe it to her and her mother, to at least try.

I scoop her up awkwardly, best I can with my one good arm, cringing at the angle at which her head flops and pray that I am not causing further damage by moving her. I settle her into the truck bed next to my bike and collect my bow, and the desert eagle, which I find I'm now rather fond of. Luckily the truck is an automatic, so driving with one hand should be doable. Hope hops in next to me and I lean against her broad shoulder for a moment before firing up the engine.

"Let's go home, pooch."

# Epilogue

The new sun rises, barely visible through the heavy clouds and thick, driving sheets of rain, casting weak, gray light over the carnage spread far and wide around the cold ashes of the dead campfire. Three great beasts roam the scene, nimbly stepping from body to body, blood spray to bullet hole, sniffing and tasting the air with forked tongues. Lizards it would seem, though greater in size than even Komodo dragons, and far more agile. Their limbs move almost bonelessly, in a slithering fashion more reminiscent of snakes, keeping low to the ground, bellies almost dragging on the rocks and dust as they skitter from corpse to corpse.

One of the beasts opens a set of jaws bigger than an alligator's, using them and the razor sharp teeth within to shear through the lower leg of one of the dead men, swallowing the limb whole in one, convulsive movement. A sharp whistle peals out across the gray plain and the three beasts all rise on their legs and turn to the sound, showcasing deceptive height. They peal across the ground, so fast as to only be a blur of motion and stop at the feet of a woman, flanked by a dozen or so men.

"Now now my dears. You can eat your fill when we're finished here."

Her voice is high and girlish, almost sweet in tone, the kind of voice that could either be appealing, or set your teeth on edge. She looks young, perhaps mid twenties at the oldest, but her eyes betray a soul that is much older. Her skin is smooth and solid, with a faint pattern that emerges when a rare ray of sunlight touches her. A shimmer that is similar to the scales covering her lizards, for they are clearly *her* lizards, their rapt attention now focussed entirely on her. The surrounding men eye the lizards warily, one eye on their location even as they take in the breadth of the destruction that lies before them.

She kneels before her beasts, laying her hands on two of them, touching her forehead to the third, and is completely still. The men continue to watch her, with no surprise in their expressions as she pushes back to her feet, every movement limber and well oiled, her fingers continuing to scratch the skull of the lizard at her right hand. Its eyes close like a cat being petted as she scratches absentmindedly, seeming to ponder something.

"One woman. *One woman.*" She murmurs, almost to herself. The men shift their weight uncomfortably, clearly wanting to speak, but too afraid to be the person to catch her attention. She appears calm to look at, but the wind seems to be rising around her, and the tension among the men is thickening, their fear and worry palpable. The man nearest to her opens his mouth as though to speak, but the words die in his throat as the three beasts and the woman turn to look at him simultaneously, the movements completely in sync, and now we can see her eyes and begin to understand the fear that grips this band of strong, big men. Glowing amber and slitted, like those of the animals at her feet, she stares at the man who was about to speak, unblinking, until a second eyelid sweeps its way across her eyes, snapping back into place almost too quickly to be seen. He swallows hard and closes his mouth, stepping half a pace back from her.

"Eighteen of my best men, slaughtered by a single woman. The woman you all told me I didn't need to worry about. And the child. The child is gone. I had plans for her."

Her demeanour is still calm, but her hand whips out and back in a movement so fast as to be almost invisible, and four long, deep cuts have opened on the would be speaker's throat. He croaks with surprise and drops to his knees, and the lizards are on him before his lifeblood has even cleared the wounds. Vicious, serrated claws are visible on the woman's hand for a brief moment, before retracting. The other men stand stock still, terror written on every feature as she examines each of them in turn, their comrade devoured in a matter of seconds.

"If you want something done right..." the woman turns away and snaps her fingers, giving the lizards the signal they were waiting for. The men collectively flinched as the lizards bounded towards the corpses, snapping and tearing their way through the assembled dead as the woman walks towards the rising sun. They fall in line behind her, as her words reach their ears.

"Send a woman to do it."

# **<u>The End</u>**

13036087R00099

Printed in Great Britain
by Amazon